EPIC

ADVENTURE

(Kind of)

By
Liz Pichon

Not very

secret stuff

↓

Scholastic Children's Books
An imprint of Scholastic Ltd
Euston House, 24 Eversholt Street,
London, NW1 1DB, UK
Registered office: Westfield Road, Southam,
Warwickshire, CV47 0RA
SCHOLASTIC and associated logos are trademarks
and/or registered trademarks of Scholastic Inc.

First published in the UK by Scholastic Ltd, 2017
This edition published 2018
Text copyright © Liz Pichon, 2017
The right of Liz Pichon to be identified as the author and illustrator
of this work has been asserted by her.

ISBN 978 1407 1 6808 1

A CIP catalogue record for this book
is available from the British Library.

Printed by CPI Group (UK) Ltd, Croydon, CR0 4YY
Papers used by Scholastic Children's Books are made
from wood grown in sustainable forests.

1 3 5 7 9 10 8 6 4 2

www.scholastic.co.uk

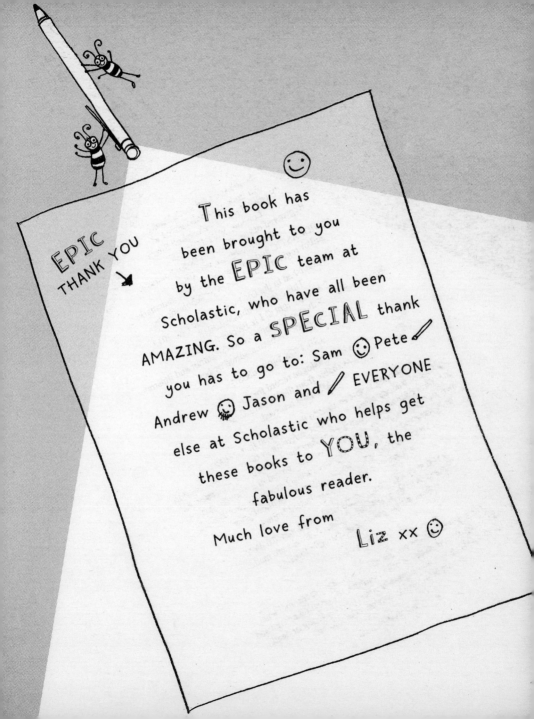

EPIC
THANK YOU →

This book has been brought to you by the EPIC team at Scholastic, who have all been AMAZING. So a SPECIAL thank you has to go to: Sam ☺ Pete Andrew ☻ Jason and ✏ EVERYONE else at Scholastic who helps get these books to YOU, the fabulous reader.

Much love from

Liz xx ☺

Ever since my grandparents came back from travelling around the WORLD, I've seen a LOT more of them.

Mostly because they've rented a flat just round the corner from our house, which I think is BRILLIANT! Dad doesn't seem quite so pleased.

REALLY? That near?

I've been finding out lots of things about them too. Who knew OLD people could be SO

BENDY?

Mum and I have come round to see how Granny Pet and Granddad Joe are settling in. We weren't expecting to see them upside down, on the floor ...

... doing YOGA.

We learned these moves in **INDIA**,

Granddad Joe tells me,

crossing and uncrossing his legs.

"It's good for keeping you flexible," Granny Pet

says while balancing on her head.

"It seems to be working for you!"

Mum agrees.

"Why don't you do YOGA, Mum?" I ask.

"Because I do other things, like look after

you lot," she says.

I show The Wrinklies (that's their nickname)

how to pat their tummies and rub their heads at

the same time.

"It looks easy, but if you don't concentrate you can get in a muddle."

"A bit like YOGA," Granddad Joe says, swapping his legs over again.

Granny Pet manages to do it, but Granddad Joe gives up because he says it's MESSING up his hair.

I also discover that The Wrinklies can speak FOUR different languages.

"You two are FULL of surprises!" Mum says, because she didn't know that either.

How do you say YOU ARE AN IDIOT in ANY language that Delia won't understand?

I want to know, as that will be useful and FUN to try out.

He! He! He! What did you say?

"I'm not sure Delia understands English sometimes," Mum sighs. "Why don't you learn to say something NICER instead, like 'I love my family and I want to tidy my room' in Spanish?"

Mum thinks she's HILARIOUS.

Then Granny Pet says something that neither of us understand.

> Любов и Мир. Paz y amor.

Granddad translates for us and they both do a HEART ♥ sign. "It means 'peace and love' in Russian and Spanish."

I do it back to them (the heart sign, not the Russian or Spanish bit).

▭▭▭➤ ♥ ⟵▭▭▭

We're about to leave when Granny Pet asks me about my band. "What's it called and who's in it with you?"

"It's called **DOGZOMBIES!** There's me - obviously - Derek and my friend Norman, who's a brilliant drummer as long as he hasn't had any ⬗▤⬗ SWEETS," I explain.

"DOGZOMBIES! I LOVE that name! That reminds me, we brought something back from South Africa that you could use in the band. It's still packed away so we'll bring it round next time we see you."

I'm excited about THAT.

YES!

THEN Mum only goes and TELLS The Wrinklies that they DON'T HAVE to keep giving us gifts all the time.

"Honestly, you being HOME is the best present EVER, isn't it, Tom?"

"Errrrrrrr, yes ... but I still like getting presents," I add, just so they know how I feel. Mum gives me a ⊜⊜ LOOK, which changes pretty FAST when Granddad shows her some fancy sunglasses from France that he's bought her. She puts them on straight away.

(So much for no more presents.)

Then Granny Pet says, "We got something else for you too, Tom - nothing BIG."

Which is a nice surprise.

It's a

DIGITAL WATCH

with special gadgets

AND an **ALARM** on it too.

"So you'll never be late for school or band practice again!" Granny Pet says.

"HOW FANTASTIC! It's like a SPY WATCH from a FILM! What do you say, Tom?"

"I **LOVE** IT! Thank you!"

I TEST OUT some of the buttons on the WATCH.

The NOISES are LOUDER than I expected.

Good **FUN** though.

Oh great...

BUZZ

BUZZZ

BUZZ

BUZZ BUZZ

RING RING

RING RING

On the way home I discover LOADS of other things the watch can do. I show them to Mum, who doesn't seem quite as KEEN as she was before. The BARKING DOG sound is VERY realistic, and so is the cow mooing. The ALARM BELL is good too. There are so many to choose from. I can't WAIT to show Derek.

He's going to LOVE my watch, I bet!

"Whooooaaaaaaaaaaaaaaaaa!"

(Derek loves my watch.)

I get to demonstrate what

it does as we're walking to school

the next day.

STRAIGHT AWAY Derek takes

out one of his SPY BOOKS

to show me.

"LOOK, he's wearing a watch

like yours on the COVER!"

"Oh yeah..." I say, pretending it's the same.

(It's not.)

I'm going to borrow Derek's SPY books when

he's finished reading them as they look really good.

I nearly walk into a LAMP POST while demonstrating

the THUNDER CLAP sound effect. →

Derek LAUGHS.

"You need a HAIRCUT."

Then he points to an ACTUAL hairdresser's we're walking past and says ⬇ I should go in THERE.

"NO WAY! That's where Granny Mavis has her hair done," I say, but then we notice that, standing in the RIGHT place, we can see OUR reflections in the hairstyle photos.

"Do you like my hair?" Derek says, which is HILARIOUS!

There's one photo that reminds me of a haircut Dad gave me by accident when he put the hair clippers on a LOW setting.

Just a trim.

(It was VERY short.)

"Look at THAT ONE! Who'd have a haircut like THAT?" Derek says, standing in front of the PHOTO, and we have a good LAUGH.

While we're messing around, I check my watch and realize we've been outside HAIRTASTIC longer than we probably should have, and THAT'S when there's a knock at the window.

Knock Knock

"Was that you?" Derek asks.

"No, I thought it was YOU."

Then a lady opens the door...

 "Can I help you boys or are you
on your way to school?"

 School, we both say and get going.

"That's the lady in the PHOTO," Derek whispers.

"I'm never having a haircut THERE!" I say.

"Me neither," Derek agrees.

BEEP! BEEP! BEEP!

My watch ALARM goes off as I walk into class. Marcus is already there, sitting down. I'm about to show him my WATCH when he says,

"Have you been invited?"

"To what?" I say.

He ignores me and leans back in his chair to ask **AMY**. "You've got one, haven't you?"

"Yes, I do." **AMY** shows us her envelope.

(I don't have one of those envelopes.)

"It's Julia Morton's birthday this weekend and she's having an ADVENTURE PARTY at a boating lake. ARE YOU COMING?" Marcus asks me.

"I'm not sure," I tell him, because I haven't had an invitation ... yet.

"I'm sure you're invited," **AMY** says to make me feel better.

Marcus keeps waving his envelope around like a FLAG. "You don't want to MISS OUT on this party," he laughs.

"Yeah, it sounds like **FUN** ..."

I'm trying to be positive and not worry about the LACK of a party invitation.

"Do you want me to ask Julia where your invitation is?" **AMY** asks.

"No, it's OK, don't worry," I say just as

M r F ullerman tells Marcus to put down his envelope.

That goes for ALL of you. PLEASE put them AWAY.

When Mr Fullerman says **"ALL of YOU..."**
it sounds like the WHOLE class behind me are
putting their *invitations* away.

It doesn't matter.

Who wants to go to a party anyway?

(I do.) ☹

Thanks to a really good SCIENCE lesson I
manage NOT to think about the party TOO much.
Mr Fullerman does an impressive experiment to
make a VOLCANO.

We all have to stand WAY back when he makes
the volcano **ERUPT**...

The *FUN* part is watching the experiment — the HARD part is writing down what happened.

(Some of this drawing is made up.)

I'm busy finishing off my **SCIENCE** drawing when my watch **ALARM** goes off (again). It's set to a **COW MOOING,** which confuses Marcus.

Huh?

MOOOO MOOOO MOOOO

Mr Fullerman doesn't look too happy either as I can't turn it off. I pretend the **MOOING** has nothing to do with me and am saved by the real bell for break time.

Ding
Ding

MOOOO
MOOOO
MOOOO

My watch has been a good distraction from thinking about the party, until Marcus asks me another QUESTION.

"Is **D**erek going to Julia's party?"

"I don't know, Marcus. He isn't in our class, so probably NOT," I say. Then I press the dog barking noise, which makes him jump.

WOOF
WOOF
WOOF

Huh?

The FIRST thing Derek asks me when I see him is,

Are you going to Julia Morton's party?

No, I'm not invited.

Why not?

Maybe she has enough kids already?

Derek thinks she probably just forgot to bring my *invitation* in with her.

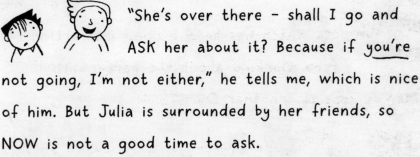

"She's over there – shall I go and ASK her about it? Because if _you're_ not going, I'm not either," he tells me, which is nice of him. But Julia is surrounded by her friends, so NOW is not a good time to ask.

If I'm not invited, I don't want EVERYONE to know.

"It's OK, Derek, don't do that. I'm FINE," I say.

(I'm not fine.)

I spend the rest of the day trying NOT to think about it (which isn't easy).
This afternoon we're doing POETRY, and making our own HAIKU poems.
They are supposed to have three lines and be very meaningful.

Sigh

I'm going to a party.

You been invited?

While I'm writing my poem, Marcus asks me about the party AGAIN.

"No invite yet," I say like I'm NOT worried.
AMY hears and she says, "What? Julia STILL hasn't asked you?"

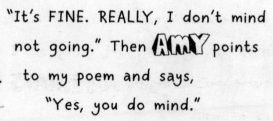

"It's FINE. REALLY, I don't mind not going." Then AMY points to my poem and says, "Yes, you do mind."

I'm **NOT** invited

To the really fun party

How bad is that? (BAD)

Marcus reads my poem out LOUD in a SAD voice.

No need.

"Cheer up, Tom, it might be a **RUBBISH** party. All we're doing is going to the BOATING **LAKE** and the adventure playground and then having a PICNIC, with games, presents and FUN. You won't be missing anything. OH, hang on, I forgot – someone's bringing **ANIMALS** to show us as well."

"ANIMALS! REALLY?

Thanks for telling me, Marcus. I feel **SO** much better now."

Then I see HIS poem, which is a

bit different to mine.

Smug mug →

BRIGHT morning sunshine

Smiling kids at the party

Apart from just ONE

"Did you have to write that?" I ask Marcus.

"I feel **BAD** that you're the ONLY kid not invited," he tells me, which is funny because

he doesn't look like he

feels bad for me.

Party

Party

Party

Mr Fullerman wants to make an announcement, so he stands up and CLAPS to get our attention.

(We clap back.)

"I know how much you ENJOY a spelling test, so we've got another one coming up soon. I'm giving you LOTS of time to learn the WORD list. Don't forget your stories too."

He points to a BIG PILE of paper on his DESK, which makes me GROAN.

Then AMY NUDGES me.

"Don't GROAN - I have good news. Julia's found your *invitation* in her bag. She's going to make sure you get it."

AMY has only sorted EVERYTHING OUT while I've been listening and watching Marcus being smug.

I'm SO HAPPY ☺

I want to get up and **CHEER**. (I don't.)
I do an AIR punch instead.

I turn around and see Julia with my *invitation* in her
hand. But then she only goes and PASSES it to...

BRAD GALLOWAY! (Oh, no...)

He treats my envelope like
some kind of Frisbee
and instead of passing it
to ME, he only goes and

FLICKS *it into*

... and my HAND. Then it HITS Mr Fullerman's desk and LANDS on the FLOOR.

Julia GASPS and Brad mouths Sorry to me.

Mr Fullerman LOOKS UP, like he knows SOMETHING is going on. He narrows his eyes, STARES at us, and then goes back to his work. I can SEE my envelope for a few moments before Mr Fullerman PUTS HIS FOOT ON IT!

 NO!

GET OFF MY *invitation!* (I think.)

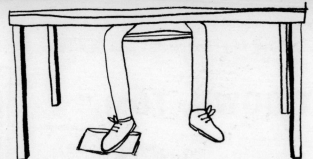

Mr Fullerman then asks if we've all enjoyed
writing these poems.

"Yes, sir," the class reply.

Mr Fullerman's foot hasn't BUDGED,

so I accidentally-on-purpose DROP my

pen on the floor.

"You've dropped your pen," Marcus says helpfully.

"I know. I'm picking it up," I whisper, then

I EDGE CLOSER on my hands and knees towards

my envelope.

For a moment, Mr Fullerman moves his foot ...
but then he PUTS it back AGAIN.

So I wait a bit LONGER...

I try pulling the envelope just a little...

"SIT DOWN, TOM."

Yes, sir...

Mr Fullerman PICKS up my *invitation* and puts it ON his table, and I have to go back to my DESK. (With my pen.)

"Your envelope's on his table now," Marcus tells me.

"I <u>know</u>," I sigh just as Mr Fullerman GETS UP and walks to the BACK of the classroom.

THIS IS MY CHANCE!

"I'm going to get it..." I tell Marcus.

"I HAVE to see THIS," he says like he doesn't think I'll do it.

I LEAN over the DESK with a ruler and LIFT it UP. Then SOMEHOW I manage to GRAB the envelope

[despite Marcus prodding me with HIS ruler].

"YES! GOT IT!" I say.

HOORAY! AT LAST.

"Told you Julia had just forgotten,"

AMY reminds me. (TRUE.)

We have to write another HAIKU - but THIS time my poem is a LOT more JOLLY than before.

Warm sunshine on me
I have an invitation
I am happy now

I tell Marcus that I'm DEFINITELY going.

"I've got my *invitation*. SEE?"

"Hmmmm. **NOT** really."

"What do you mean? Julia's invited me."

"Julia's invited Trevor," Marcus tells me.

(I hadn't read the front.)

Trevor must have mine. I'll have to wait until the
END of class now before we can do a SWAP. But I
AM going – that's the main thing.

I CAN'T WAIT!

Getting my *invitation* was the
HARD PART. Going to the party
will be a **LOT** easier and so much more FUN too.

What else could go wrong?

PLEASE COME TO MY
ADVENTURE PARTY

TOM

We're meeting at the LAKE at the park, then
going BOATING! There'll be FUN, food, games
and a visit from some animal friends as well.
Details on the back.
Please RSVP.
Love, Julia

Not long now...

Julia Morton's BIRTHDAY★PARTY

You never know what a PARTY is going to be like until you arrive. There are lots of reasons why a party might NOT go exactly to plan – kids getting ill,

I feel sick

people not turning up,

or too many people turning up. →

My parties have always been **AMAZING**, even the ones Delia tried to MESS up when I was younger.

Delia

Ross White  in my class had a CLOWN party once. All the kids were happily playing "pin the ◉↤nose on the clown" when the REAL clown turned up. Which would have been OK, if he hadn't **LEAPT** out and shouted,

SURPRISE! WHERE'S THE BIRTHDAY BOY?

AGH!

Ross got a big **SHOCK** and lots of kids screamed and ran away. The birthday CAKE was a BIG WEIRD clown face too, but we got over that because who doesn't like CAKE? I'm sure Julia's party is going to be <u>EXCELLENT</u>.

(With no clowns.) ☺

Dad offered to give my friends a lift to the boating lake, so Derek, Norman and Solid have all come to my house first.

I'll drive you all.

Mum says, "Who'd like a quick snack to keep you going?" Which is a SURPRISE.

She keeps trying to smooth my hair down as well. "It's in your EYES, Tom. You need a HAIRCUT!"

Mum! I say, hoping she'll STOP fussing.

The "SNACKS" turn out to be GRAPES. "There'll be PLENTY of party food later," Mum tells us.

(I hope so.)

My friends eat a few grapes and because Mum is watching me, I do as well.

I notice that Derek's bought Julia a very BIG present.

"What is it?" I ask.

"I don't know. Dad bought it and wrapped it up and I forgot to ask," he says, still eating grapes. Derek gives it a good "SHAKE" and nothing rattles, so it's not broken.

"What if it's something EMBARRASSING?" Norman points out.

"I'll blame it on Dad," Derek says. Then Solid tells us HE got given a WHISK once.

"Did you want a whisk?" I wonder.

"Not really, but I pretended I did." Mum's listening to our conversation and LAUGHING.

"Well done, Solid. You're ALL very lucky to get presents and go to parties!" she points out.

(Granny Mavis gave me embarrassing pants once - I don't mention those.)

Cuddly toy pants

Shudder

Solid has got Julia a book token and a **FUNNY** card. Norman's giving her a **CHOCOLATE MONEY box** and CHOCOLATE MONEY, which I like the sound of.  (Yum.)

I show everyone **my NEW WATCH.** →

Derek's seen it already and tells them it's my **SPY WATCH.**

"Kind of ... but would a **SPY WATCH** do this?" I say, and I press the **COW MOOING** sound to prove a point.

"Yes! If you were hiding in a FIELD of COWS, it would be very useful," Derek says.

 Then Mum tells me NOT to start pressing **ALL** the buttons again.

"Save it for the CAR JOURNEY," she says, smiling.

 Solid wants to know what I've got for Julia.

"It's a REALLY brilliant colouring book AND some fantastic pens too. They're GREAT to USE – with LOTS of nice colours. When you're colouring in there are so many to choose from."

 "How do you know, Tom? You haven't started colouring Julia's book, have you? It's HER present, not YOURS!"

"Ummmmmmmmmmm...

No... Not really."

(Maybe a little.)

CAKES AND CATS

SOCKS AND STARS

Once I'd started, it was hard to stop.

"**R**ight – who's READY for an **ADVENTURE** PARTY?"

Dad asks, which is good timing as now

Mum can't check Julia's present.

Once we're in the car, Dad tells

JOKES all the way to the boating lake.

Keen

What's orange and sounds like a parrot?

A carrot!

Groan

After every joke

I PRESS

my DIGITAL WATCH and

BLOW raspberries, which makes

my friends "LAUGH" more

than Dad's jokes do.

RRASSSSPPPPP
RRRRRRAAAAASSSSPPPP
RRASSSSPPPPP
RRASSSSPPPP

When we arrive, Julia's dad (who looks like Julia

with a beard) asks MY dad if he'd like to stay for

the party. He wasn't planning to hang around but

when he sees the grown-ups' food ...

I will!

Help yourself!

Weird crisps

Avocado and Ketchup with Pepper

... he doesn't need much persuading.

My stomach's grumbling already, but there's no time to follow Dad, as we're taken down to the boating lake. Julia waves at us, and lots of our classmates are already there – including Marcus (who's not waving).

There's a group of girls that I don't recognize at all. "They're my friends from camping club," Julia tells us. (Who knew Julia went camping?) Marcus asks her what they DO at camping club and she says,

"Errr ... CAMP and play games." Which sounds **FUN**. (Though Mum told Dad she's not going camping again – EVER.)

Julia helps hand out life jackets, but as I'm putting mine on I don't hear everything the boating instructor is telling us.

"Get into PAIRS and put on your life jackets. Now, remember, stay safe, don't stand up in the boat, don't get into the lake, NO SPLASHING and stick to the SIGNPOSTED areas. We'll come and get you if there's a problem. Are there any questions?"

"Is there ANYTHING in the WATER that can **BITE?**" Julia asks.

Someone (Brad Galloway) thinks it's funny to shout out, "SHARKS!"

"NO sharks or anything that can do you any harm," the instructor assures us ALL.

Phew.

Then Mark Clump only goes and tells us about snapping PIKE fish, insects that BITE  and RATS that swim.

They're probably out there NOW. You should be OK - BUT don't put your hand in the WATER.

SNAP

"Like I said... You'll all be FINE. Now you're in your PAIRS, let's get into your BIRD BOATS!"

Somehow, by standing NEXT to Marcus I've been
PAIRED with him. I don't complain,
though, as it's Julia's party after all.
It won't be for **long**.

"I'll be in charge of making the
bird go in the right direction," Marcus tells me.

"Fine," I say, because I just want to get going.
The BIRD BOATS have pedals and a rudder at the
back to STEER them with. But when it's time to
get into OUR boat, it looks DIFFERENT
to everyone else's... More like a worm
than a bird.

"It's exactly the same as the
others — it's just missing a beak,"
the instructor tells us.

We get in and straight away Marcus makes it WOBBLE a lot.

"(M)" I can see Dad WAVING at me and still eating crisps.

"OK, boys, OFF you go!" The instructor *pushes* us out. Marcus is in CHARGE of steering the bird in a STRAIGHT LINE. Only he doesn't.

"Make it go *FORWARDS!*" he tells me.

"It's <u>YOU</u> - you're not steering it properly!" I say. We're going round and round in circles, so I STOP pedalling.

"Why have <u>you</u> STOPPED?" Marcus says. "Keep going."

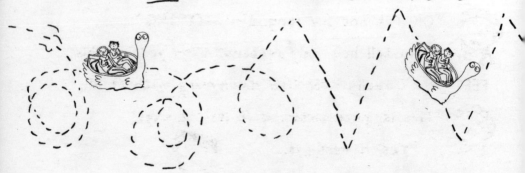

We ZIGZAG from one side to another.

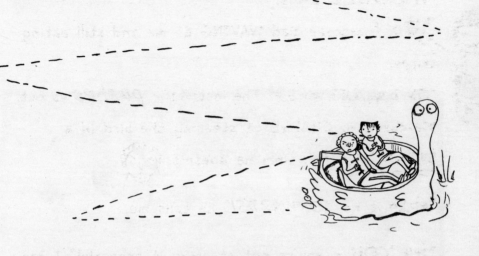

I'm getting tired of doing all the work.

"Come on, Marcus, if you help out we'll go FASTER,"

I tell him.

"OK, but not for long. I'm STEERING."

I can tell he's only pretending to pedal as his

FEET aren't really PUSHING down very much at all.

"This is quite tiring, isn't it?" he says.

"Yes, it really is..."

Sigh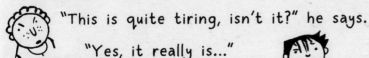

We FINALLY start moving in a straight line when Marcus says, "That island looks interesting. Let's go there."

"OK, but don't go TOO CLOSE," I say.

For some reason Marcus suddenly decides that
NOW is a good time to start PEDALLING.

Our bird boat ====SHOOTS

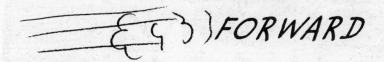

FORWARD

and before we can stop or turn in a different

direction, we get

WELL

AND

TRULY...

STUCK.

"Which part of 'don't get too close' did you not understand?" I ask Marcus, who says, "IT WASN'T MY FAULT!" (It was.)

Lots of the other kids pedal past us and wave.

(Brilliant.)

Then Marcus decides that he wants something to **eat** and brings out a SANDWICH from his pocket.

"Don't eat that NOW!" I tell him.

"Why not? I'm hungry?"

"It's <u>only</u> a SANDWICH. We could be here for **AGES**," Marcus moans.

(I really hope not.)

His sandwich attracts a lot of birds, who start swimming towards us.

"*SHOOO, SHOOO,*" Marcus says, trying to stop them from pecking his food.

"They want your sandwich," I tell him.
We're completely surrounded by birds now.

"It's MINE - they can't have it."

"These birds are NOT getting my food," Marcus says ...

... just before a bird swoops down and ...
TAKES IT!

"HEY, that's MY SANDWICH!"

he shouts as the bird flies away.

"Not any more, it's not," I mutter.
I remind Marcus that there'll be
food at the party, but he's NOT
happy at ALL.

Neither is the boating instructor,
who has to row out to rescue us.

"There's always ONE – or TWO, in your case –
who don't read the signs. Didn't you see it said
SHALLOW WATER?"

"Obviously not," Marcus says, which actually
makes me LAUGH.

The SAME BIRD flies past Marcus and he tries to splash it with water, which lands all over us instead.

"MARCUS!"

I shout and the lady tells us both, "NO splashing WATER, you TWO!"

"It wasn't ME!" I say.

"I'm soaked," Marcus says, like it wasn't his fault. As we're being towed back some kids WAVE and point, while I look straight ahead and pretend that this isn't happening.

I can see Dad waiting for us. He helps me climb out of the boat with one hand while FILMING our rescue with the other.

"Smile, boys! Are you having a good TIME?" he asks us on camera.

"What do you think, Dad?"

Embarrassing wet patches →

He keeps filming as we walk towards him.

"Oh dear, you're both a bit WET – like two monsters from the DEEP LAGOON! If you run around you'll dry off faster," Dad suggests while trying not to LAUGH. (He's full of good advice.)

The sun does dry us off a little, which is something, and we finally get to sit down and have a party **box** lunch and a few other snacks too – which is just as well as I get a 𝕥𝕦𝕟𝕒 sandwich in mine.

I swap it with Solid, who gives me his biscuit.

(It's a very good SWAP, so I'm happy.)

One of Julia's friends asks me if that's my dad over there.

"YES..." I say, watching him balance boxes on his head.

"He's really FUNNY," she tells me, as the party boxes fall off on to the floor.

"Sometimes," I sigh.

Whoa!

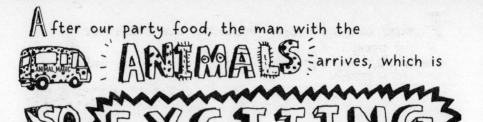

After our party food, the man with the ANIMALS arrives, which is

SO EXCITING.

All the kids get up and RUSH over to see what he's going to show us. I grab EXTRA BISCUITS, so I'm a bit slow getting there. The man is talking about LONG-EARED BUNNIES and there are lots of "ooooooohs" and "ahhhhhhhhs" going on. The BIG problem for me is that I'm right at the BACK of the group and lots of kids' HEADS are in my way. When the man brings out a corn snake, I don't get to see THAT properly either.

I miss out on seeing ALL of the creatures until FINALLY he brings out something called an ARMADILLO,* which is curled up in a ball and fast asleep.

"You might have noticed the ARMADILLO has very tough skin covered in scales, and an UNUSUAL ODOUR." Lots of kids take a step back – which is my chance to move forwards. "Who wants to HOLD IT?"

I DO!

I shout and wave my arms around so the man PICKS ME!

"Can you sit down and cup your hands together? Don't drop him," the man tells me. Then he passes the ARMADILLO over to me ... very gently ...

*See a real armadillo on page 224-225

... and that's when the

SMELL hits me.

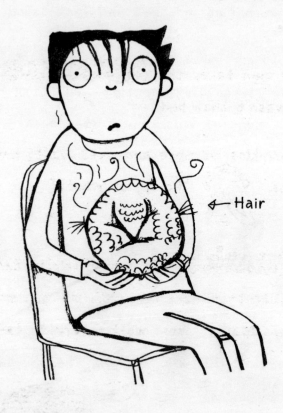

← Hair

I try to stay still and breathe through my mouth as much as possible.

Dad keeps taking photos and telling me to smile.
I do my best.

Dad says I look surprised and **DISGUSTED** at the
same time.

When the man takes the ARMADILLO back, I
say, "It wasn't that bad."

Marcus wrinkles his nose and does wafty hand
movements.　　"Pongy or what?"

"The ARMADILLO is probably thinking EXACTLY the
same thing about you!" the man with the animals says,
which stops Marcus from wafting pretty fast.

Kids...

When it's time to go home, Julia hands out the PARTY BAGS, then she decides to open a few presents before we all leave as well.

"This one's from Norman. Wow, chocolate! I love chocolate!" she says.

"ME TOO!" Norman agrees.

Next she opens Derek's present, so he gets to find out what it actually is. "How did you know? I've always wanted SEA MONKEYS!" Julia tells him in a really excited voice.

"I guessed!" Derek smiles. Then Julia picks up my present and I say, "NO, you don't have to open it now - really."

But it's too late.

Uh-oh...

"Thanks, Tom. Pens and a colouring book!" Julia starts flicking through the pages.

"You've already done some of the colouring for me... That's great! I can copy your pages. Thanks, Tom." Julia seems pleased I've started the book for her.

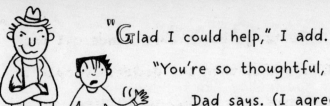

"Glad I could help," I add.

"You're so thoughtful, Tom!"
Dad says. (I agree.)

We all say BYE and thank Julia and her family for the party. Then we jump in the car with our PARTY BAGS. (I've discovered pink shrimps in mine!)

Derek, Norman and Solid all bring out a **SECRET AGENT PEN** SPY PEN with invisible ink from their bags. "We can write secret messages in class!" Norman says.

"Have you got one, Tom?" Derek asks.

I keep looking but the only thing I find is ...

... a YO-YO with a silly face.

"That's what you looked like holding the ARMADILLO, Tom!" Dad says and my friends all LAUGH.

"It did pong a bit," I tell them while eating a pink shrimp.

When Dad stops at some traffic lights he says, "Tell me when the light goes green." Then, while I'm not looking, he pinches a shrimp.

The second time,

Dad!

I CATCH him.

As we drop everyone back home, they all wave goodbye (( )) while holding their

SECRET AGENT PENS,

which makes me want one EVEN MORE.

Derek says he MIGHT have an old one at his house that I can have, which would be ACE.

"We can write SECRET NOTES that no one else can read," Derek tells me, then adds, "apart from your grandparents, who are SPIES, of course."

"Ha! I don't think so," I say. I'd forgotten Derek thinks The Wrinklies are SPIES...

When I get home Mum's chatting with Delia in the kitchen. Straight away Delia points at my still slightly damp trousers and says, "Did you have an ACCIDENT, Tom?"

"NO. Marcus SPLASHED me with LAKE WATER," I say quickly so she can't make any more jokes.

"Yeah, right."

"What was the party like?" Mum wants to know.

"It was OK," I say, looking round for my PARTY BAG, which has disappeared.

"Did you enjoy yourself?" she asks.

"Kind of - but not as much as Dad did..."

I point to Dad,
who's got my PARTY BAG.

It's been ages
since I had a go
with a yo-yo!

The GOOD NEWS is that Derek has FOUND his spare  SECRET AGENT PEN.

I set my alarm to the CAR BEEP noise so I can wake up nice and early and get it from him before school tomorrow.

Things are looking UP!

I'm woken up by  GOOSE HONKING.

HONK
HONK
HONK

(Not a car beeping like I expected.)

I press my watch a few times outside Delia's room just for *FUN* before I go to school.

Go away, Tom.

Derek gives me the PEN straight away, which is a GOOD START to the day.

YES!

Thanks, Derek.

When we get to school Mr Keen is saying "Hello" and "Morning" to everyone.

"Hello, Derek, and who's that with you? Oh, it's you, Tom! I couldn't see your face. Your hair is all over your EYES!"

Hello, sir.

(It's not that long.)

I'm walking to class and pushing my hair out of my eyes when I SPOT a BIG new poster on the school noticeboard. Derek and I STOP to READ it and accidentally create a bit of a jam in the corridor.

SCHOOL TR🙂PICAL
DISC🙂

Get ready for some SCORCHING TUNES!
Money raised goes towards the school library.
FOR YEARS 5 and 6.
Dress for HOT weather.

IT'S SUMMERTIME at OAKFIELD SCHOOL!

Then **Buster Jones** comes along and starts
telling everyone, "KEEP GOING!
CORRIDOR MONITOR coming through.
Who's holding everyone up?"

(That'll be us, then.)

"Oh, it's you, Gatesy. I didn't recognize
you with the long hair."

"It's not THAT long," I tell him.

He looks at the poster on the wall and says,

"what do you THINK?"

Derek and I wonder if it's a trick question, but
we both say we like it. (Just in case.)

"Did you do it, **Buster?**" I ask.

"NO, of course not. But I've added a few
things, if you GET ME. Shhhhhhh!

Don't say a word." We won't.

Looking at the poster* again, it takes me a while to see what **Buster's** been up to. He's got a bit of a reputation in school, but he's always OK with us. I think the teachers give him lots of JOBS to keep him busy and stop him getting into mischief. It hasn't worked this time, though. **Mr S**procket is here (and dancing), so **Buster** goes into CORRIDOR MONITOR voice again.

"MOVE, EVERYONE! You too, Gatesy."

Derek goes off to class and we arrange to meet up and swap **SECRET MESSAGES** later. I can hear **Buster** saying,

NOTHING TO SEE HERE. IT'S JUST A POSTER FOR A TROPICAL DISCO, THAT'S ALL. HURRY UP!

I know he's not talking to ME, but his voice still makes me go faster.

* See close-up of poster on page 222

Marcus is already in his seat, and it doesn't take long for him to remind me about Julia's party.

(And not in a good way.)

"It wasn't my fault we got stuck!" he tells me (even though it was).

"If you say so, Marcus," I sigh.

"HEY, I got a **SECRET AGENT PEN** in my **PARTY** bag. What did you get?" he wants to know while showing off his pen.

"A yo-yo..." Marcus doesn't look that impressed.

"I'm glad I got this **PEN.** I've been writing **SECRET MESSAGES** with it." He shows me a **BLANK** piece of paper.

"WOW – that looks very important," I say jokingly.

"It _IS_. That's why you can't see it."

"Oh, but I can!" I tell him and I take out my pen and shine my torch on it. Marcus takes it away quickly. "It's **SECRET!**"

AMY sits down and asks us both if we're going to the TROPICAL **disco**.

"I'm going – it sounds fun, just like Julia's party was!" she says happily.

"I'M GOING TOO!"

I say a bit loudly.

"Calm down, Tom," Marcus tells me.

I still have my **SECRET AGENT PEN** out, so while **Mr** Fullerman is calling out the register, I take a sneaky look at Marcus's **SECRET NOTE** with my torch.

I LIKE SANDWICHES. Not BIRDS.

(It's not much of a BIG secret, if you ask me.)

I do a few of my own **SECRET MESSAGES**, which I show to Derek after school ...

... and keep away from teachers and Marcus.

June's dad (our next-door neighbour) is in the band **Plastic Cup.** But ever since their reunion didn't exactly go to plan, he's been miserable. I know this because I can hear him singing really **GLOOMY** songs through my bedroom wall.

Derek's dad told us the band kept arguing about "musical differences" all the time and then they decided not to go on tour, which Derek's dad was really sad about.

> I'm sad.

That's when all the **gloomy** singing started.

He's doing it now...

*See page 230 for message

I get Dad to come and have a listen.
"Oh dear, that sounds grim.
He probably doesn't even know you
can hear him. I'll have a little word if
it keeps you awake," Dad assures me.
We keep listening as he sings the same
thing OVER and OVER again.

 I'm starting to know it off by heart...

Plastic Cup
Plastic Cup
Where did it all go wrong?
(Everywhere)
Plastic Cup
Plastic Cup
We'll write another song
(No chance)
Plastic Cup
Plastic Cup

We're too old to fight

(We're not)

Plastic Cup

Plastic Cup

Everything will be all right

(It won't)

 When he EVENTUALLY stops, Dad is relieved. "Phew. At least <u>NOW</u> you can get some sleep, Tom."

You'd think so,

BUT I can't get the **TUNE** out of my

 **HEAD.**

Every time I close my eyes all I can do is count **plastic cups** jumping

over fences - when it should be sheep. ➔

I keep trying.

Wakey, wakey!

My watch alarm goes **off** and it's some
kind of **FOGHORN.**

It's a bit loud, but it does
the trick. I'm awake.

I might try and find a slightly LESS VICIOUS

sound for tomorrow.

When I go to brush my teeth I notice that Delia is

still in BED.

Luckily, I am a GOOD BROTHER

and I don't want her to sleep in and be

late, so I press my **FOGHORN**

button right outside her room until I can

hear she's awake.

TOM!

"I've got a DAY OFF!"

Delia shouts at me through the door.

(How was I supposed to know?)

I escape to the safety of the bathroom just in case she actually does get up. My hair **is** getting a bit LONG and keeps falling in my eyes while I'm brushing my teeth.

I spot Mum's special hair stuff on the shelf, and even though I know she gets **CROSS** if anyone uses it,

THIS ⟹ is an EMERGENCY.

I put some on and rub it in, which seems to do the trick. Mum will NEVER know I've touched it as I carefully put the lid back on. I avoid Delia by

RUNNING downstairs.

Now that I can see, it's a LOT EASIER.

I'm leaving the house when Mum says, "What IS that in your hair? You look TALLER!" She tries to **pat** my head so I do a quick SWERVE and say, "NOTHING – it's just CLEAN." I can hear Mum calling after me, 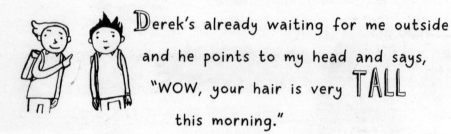 "Have you been using my HAIR PRODUCTS, TOM?" (I pretend not to hear.)

Derek's already waiting for me outside and he points to my head and says, "WOW, your hair is very TALL this morning."

"It's hair gel. I won't walk into lamp posts now."

"Good thinking – but you've got toothpaste in it too," Derek says.

It's lucky that he told me, as it's the kind of thing Marcus would notice but not say anything. He'd just LAUGH.

(It's happened before.)

Sweet paper

What?

Nothing.

When we get to school Mr Sprocket is still DANCING.

I've got the moves!

"Who's looking forward to the TR🍍PICAL **disco?**" he says as he greets us all.

I go to sit at my desk and read out what Mr Fullerman has written on the board in very BIG letters.

OH, WHAT A BEAUTIFUL MORNING!

OH, WHAT A BEAUTIFUL DAY!

I'VE GOT A WONDERFUL FEELING

THERE'S A SPELLING TEST LATER TODAY!

(IN CASE YOU'D FORGOTTEN, CLASS 5f.)

A RHYME doesn't make it any more **FUN** to do. WHY TODAY? Why not tomorrow or next week when I've had a chance to learn some of the words? Spelling tests always happen when I'm not expecting them. **M**arcus reminds me as well, in case I can't **SEE** the **GIANT** message in front of me.

"We've got a spelling test this afternoon."

 "Thanks for telling me. I don't know what I'd do without you."

"It's on the board," he adds, pointing to it.

 There is no escaping the spelling test – or Marcus – today.

I decide to use June's dad's **BAD** singing as an EXCUSE for not being able to LEARN my words because he kept me AWAKE. Idea.

It's worth a try, at least.

I put my hand up and Mr Fullerman comes over, and I have to explain everything in front of Marcus and AMY.

I do my best...

YES, TOM?

"I have a problem, sir."

"Really...?"

(I yawn for effect.) "I was kept awake ALL night by very BAD singing from my next-door neighbour, June's dad. He's in a band, and it sounded like this *ALL* night.

Plastic Cup
Plastic Cup
Where did it all go wrong?
(Everywhere)

Over and over again.

I was TRYING to learn the words for the test, but it was impossible and now all I can remember is HIS song." (I sing him a bit more to prove my point.)

I'm HOPING Mr Fullerman will instantly understand my problem and say something like...

**"Tom, that's terrible for you.
You can't possibly do your spelling
test after such a difficult night."**

Then he'll give me LOADS of
EXTRA time to practise my words. :)

But that doesn't happen.

Instead Mr Fullerman says, **"I'm sure it was bad, Tom, but the test still has to be done. I'm going to suggest you go to the library at lunchtime."**

He writes a note in my spelling book so I won't forget. (I might still try, though...)

Tom

Noisy singing is the worst.
Please go to study club
in the library at
lunchtime. The peace
and quiet will help you
learn all your words
for the spelling test
THIS AFTERNOON.

Mr Fullerman

THIS AFTERNOON is underlined several times to make a point. Marcus Meldrew reads the note over my shoulder and starts LAUGHING. Ha! Ha! Ha!

"HA! I thought you KNEW about the test? Have *FUN* in **study club**. Oh sorry ... no one has *FUN* in **study club,** do they?"

Marcus is right about that.

I don't want to spend my lunchtime at **study club**, so I make a BIG effort to get the words INTO my head by writing them out, STARING at them a lot, and memorizing each one with my EYES closed before trying to write it down.

NO looking at the answers, I tell myself.

STARE.

CLOSE EYES.

MEMORIZE.

WRITE.

AMY is watching me curiously.

 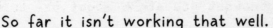 **"D**oes that help you remember them?" she wants to know.

"I'll soon find out."

So far it isn't working that well.

Marcus is making things harder by tapping his pencil on the desk next to me.

 "Do you have to do that?" I ask him.

"Do what?"

"That ... tapping."

Tap
\\\ Tap
/\\ Tap

"Sorry. I didn't know I was doing it," he says and does it some more.

"Whoops..." Marcus puts down the pencil, then taps with his ruler instead.

Tap
\\\
/\\

 THIS IS
IMPOSSIBLE.

Tap Tap

I'll have to try another way of learning my spellings, *FAST.*

If I use the words to make up a story, they MIGHT STICK in my head. Then I'll remember how to spell them too. It's worth a go. I take a GOOD LOOK at my spelling list.

CHIMNEY

CIRCUS

SPIKES

FURNITURE

UNDERSTAND

CELERY

TOMORROW

STRETCH

UNUSUAL

TOUGH

OFTEN

CACTUS

SHRIMP

GIRAFFE

Then I turn them all into a story.

I am a word genius. (True.)

Here is my story:

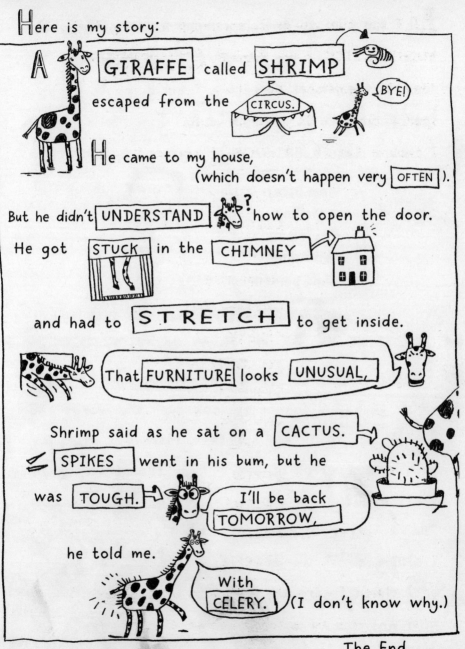

All I have to do now is remember the story and that will JOG my memory and I'll be able to spell all the words correctly. I am going to be a SPELLING MASTER.

I should make a BADGE that says:

Tom Gates
spelling
MASTER and
all-round
SMART person

I am feeling better about the test already.

In the afternoon Mr Fullerman tells us he hopes we've all had a chance to look over the words and are ready for the test. Marcus is using his HAND to cover up his work, even though we haven't started yet.

"Don't bother, Marcus. I KNOW all my words so I won't be looking at your answers," I assure him.

"We'll see. This is just in case." Marcus props up a book as well – which is a bit over the top.

I make the book fall over a few times by poking it with my pencil. It takes him a while to work out it's me doing it.

Then he puts TWO books up like he's building a wall. "I can still see your paper," I tell him, so he turns his back to me.

"Now I can see over your shoulder." I can't, but it's fun to watch him shift around like a game of HOT and COLD. I am feeling more confident about the TEST. RIGHT up until it starts.

Then things go a bit wrong.

Mr Fullerman calls out the FIRST WORD...

CACTUS.

... and my mind goes BLANK.

Errrr...   I try to remember the story
              but I can't.

And THEN I get **HICCUPS,** which doesn't help
the situation AT ALL. Mr Fullerman says it again:

"CACTUS."

 I know what a cactus looks like

but I can't remember how to spell it.

HICCUP

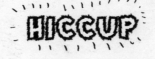

Now I've missed the next word.

Stop hiccuping!

March hisses, like I'm doing it on purpose. I'm not. HIC

I do the best I can for the rest of the test, but I'm not expecting to get an AMAZING result.

The really annoying thing is, as SOON as the test is HIC over, all the spelling words pop back into my head.

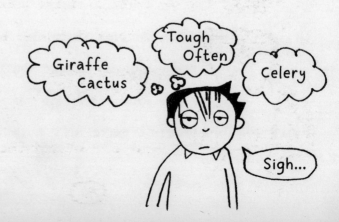

Giraffe
Cactus

Tough
Often

Celery

Sigh...

HIC I put my pen down and glance over at **AMY**'s answers.

Her page looks very different to mine, which is no **BIG SURPRISE.**

Mr Fullerman asks us to swap papers with the person next to us. Marcus takes my paper a bit too quickly for my liking.

As Mr Fullerman writes the answers on the board, Marcus keeps **HUFFING** at my spellings.

"Do you HAVE to keep **HUFFING?**" I ask him.

"**Study club** for you, I think!" he says, which is irritating, so I take my paper away from him and ask **AMY** to mark it instead. (She doesn't make ANY huffing noises.)

T hen Marcus asks **AMY** to do his paper as well.

S he sighs. "You two..."

Here's MINE.

I've had REALLY **BAD** spelling test results before, but I know this one is NOT good at all. The **HICCUPS** have stopped, so that's something.

T he **MAIN** thing I have to do NOW is make sure that this spelling paper is

NEVER EVER ...

SEEN by Mum or Dad.

Anything to show us?

Nothing to see here!

Ever. Ever, ever. (Ever.)

Mr Fullerman comes round and collects all our test results. I get a MASSIVE 5/14. 😕

I try and remind him about my late-night singing distraction AGAIN (as my excuse).

That's what study club is for, Tom! You'll remember next time.

HIC!

My hiccups come back when he says that. I decide to add a few doodles to my spelling test paper to hide my result – just in case Mum or Dad do find it.

All the crosses have nice patterns on them.

Tom Gates

(Don't judge me.)

Spelling test

1	Chimnee Chimknee
2	Cikus Sircus
3	Spikes
4	Furneture
5	Understand
6	Sellery
7	Tomorrow
8	Streetch
9	Unusual
10	Touff
11	Offten
12	Kactus
13	Shrimp
14	Jiraffe

I like to think this is an EXTRA SKILL I've learned.

(Though I'm not sure Mr Fullerman would agree.)

Meanwhile...

When I get home from school, the kitchen
is completely STUFFED full of my
FAMILY.

THE FOSSILS are getting to know The Wrinklies
a LOT more. They hang out together and have
been introducing ALL their friends to them as well
(they know a lot of people). Uncle Kevin, Aunty
Alice and the cousins are here too.

Delia isn't - she's in her room.

 whisper to Mum...

"Why's everyone here?"

"That's a very good question," she says. It's like a party (without the good food or FUN).

I wave at the cousins, who look hungry. I'm hungry too, but the cousins look hungrier.

Uncle Kevin tells us, "We got a message from Bob and Mavis to come round.

They said your parents were here too, so I left work EARLY especially."

"Gosh! Your hair's got long, Tom," he adds.

"It happens," I say.

Then Dad comes in from the shed and gets a

SURPRISE.

Whooooaaaa!

"Oh, hello! Who's won the lottery? I hope it's us!"

Granddad Bob picks up some spoons and says,

"I'll play a TUNE to celebrate!" And he does...

Clink
Clink
Clink
Clink
Clink

(I have NO idea how he does that.)
The sound sets The Wrinklies off
(sort of) DANCING. Granddad Joe's

hair is moving from side to side and I can't

help STARING at it.

Mum nudges me to STOP.

Then Delia walks in,

SEES what's going on

and leaves straight away.

What is it with my family?

It doesn't SPOIL the good mood, though.

And Granny Mavis adds to it by bringing out

a LARGE tin of biscuits.

"I made these especially for everyone!"

  I'm PLEASED but not as happy as the

cousins, who head straight for the tin.

The biscuits are HUGE!

They're more like (WHALE) biscuits than FISH ones.

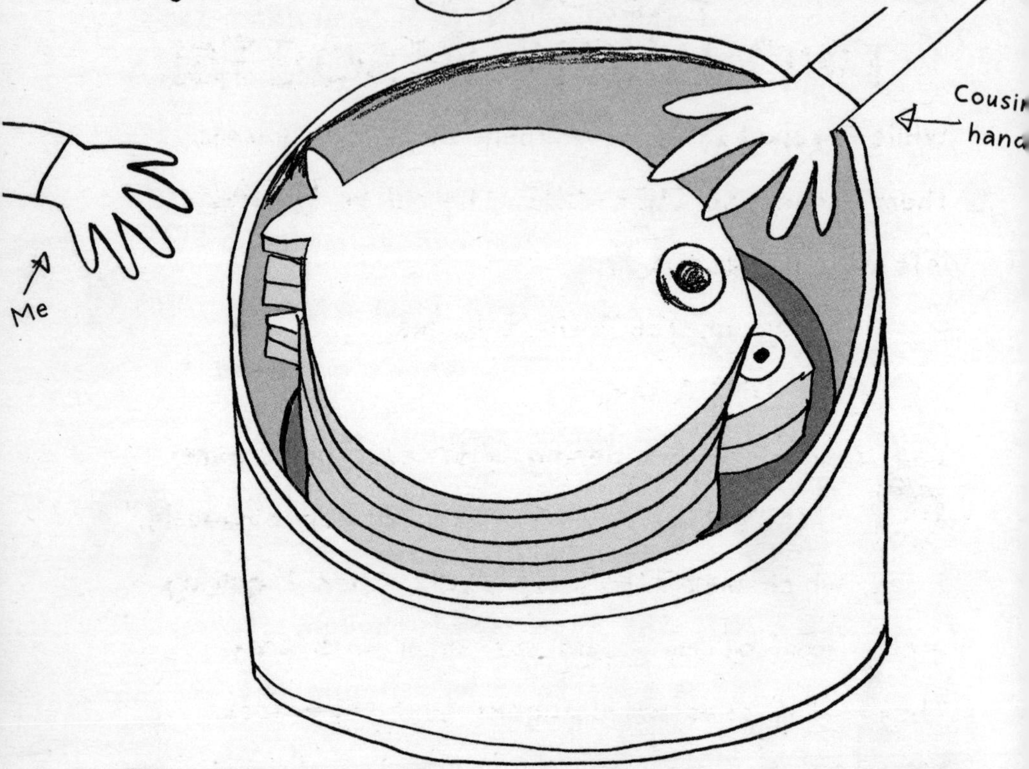

Cousin's hand

Me

I'm about to dig in when Mum stops me.

"Tom, can you give Dad a hand making some tea? Then you can have a biscuit." Awwwww.

It's ANNOYING, especially because the cousins help themselves to TWO BISCUITS EACH!

(Not one. TWO!)

TWO WHOLE BISCUITS!

While I reluctantly go to help Dad, Mum passes them around to EVERYONE. There'll be NONE left at this rate. ☹

    "Hurry up, Tom!" she tells me.

    "OK, OK," I say.

Dad is also still wondering WHY everyone's here.

    "It's because we're VERY popular, obviously," I say, which makes Dad LAUGH. Then I quickly grab a load of mugs and put them on a tray. They're the ones with slogans that Mum keeps SEPARATE from the others. Dad makes the pot of TEA and tells me, "Give THAT mug to your Uncle Kevin, Tom!"

I don't ask WHY because I want to get back to the biscuits. The hair in my eyes isn't making this easy...

My expert balancing SKILLS are put to the test when the cousins try and SPOOK me.

"TOM, DON'T DROP THEM!"

I WOBBLE a little, but they stay on the tray. Uncle Kevin takes "his" mug. He's busy REPEATING the "I swam with sharks" story (that we've all heard before but The Wrinklies haven't). Aunty Alice reminds him that he was in the aquarium – not shark-infested water.

"I'm just recounting MY adventures. Like the time I found a DEADLY spider in my... Where was it now?"

Dad says, "The zoo?" Then he points to Uncle Kevin's mug. "Just saying."
"Very funny," Uncle Kevin sighs.

At my age, I've seen it all. done it all. I just can't remember it all.

Hello, everyone!

Then The Wrinklies say they'd like to make an ANNOUNCEMENT.

"Speaking of ***ADVENTURES***, now that we're all here..." Granny Pet begins.

"Delia's in her room," I let them know.

"Don't worry. I'll take her a biscuit and go see her afterwards. I don't want her to MISS OUT," Granny Pet says. (Good luck with THAT.)

"We'd like to get the WHOLE family together and go on an ***ADVENTURE*** outing!"

"Not camping, I hope," Mum says.

"No. THIS place has lots of MAGICAL memories. It will be loads of fun."

I hear the WORD "magical" and I think I'm more excited than ever!

YES! Disneyland.

The cousins are thinking the same as me, and they each put a biscuit down to do a high-five.

"I'm glad you're so excited about **Crambly Castle**. We used to take Rita there when she was little. So many memories!" Granddad Joe tells us.

"Oh... It's hard to get <u>AS</u> excited about **CRUMBLY Castle**, although they do have a good MAZE there. Delia tried to lose me in it once.

"We thought a picnic would be nice, too!" Granny Pet adds.

"History and a picnic sounds great. Count us in!" Uncle Kevin says, even though the cousins don't seem very enthusiastic (and they've already eaten their biscuits).

But Aunty Alice is shaking her head. "Sorry, I'm refereeing a football tournament that weekend. These boys are playing and Kevin's helping with the kits."

"AM I?"

"Yes, you are. I knew you wouldn't mind," Aunty Alice tells him. "We'll do something together another time," she adds. I'm reminded of the FACT that I still haven't had a biscuit. But when I go to help myself from the tin, there's ONLY

CRUMBs LEFT.

No!

No one seems interested in my BISCUIT DISASTER. Mum asks Aunty Alice how long she's been a referee.

"I've just started, but it means I can keep an eye on these two boys!" she says and pretends to give them a red card. The cousins look thrilled. Then Granny Pet says,

"Oh, Tom, we nearly forgot..."

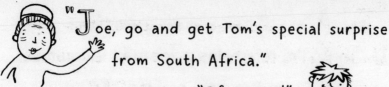

"Joe, go and get Tom's special surprise from South Africa."

"Of course!"

(It's AMAZING how quickly biscuits don't seem as important.) Yes!

"Not more presents!" Mum says, but I remind her she got those FANCY sunglasses.

"Oh, yes... OK."

Granddad Joe comes back in holding something behind his back.

"Please tell me that's NOT for Tom?"

Dad says.

"It's not for Tom," Granddad repeats. (It is for me.)

"It's called a vuvuzela, and they are VERY popular everywhere," Granny Pet says.

"Apart from here..." Dad mutters.

"Thank you! I've NEVER had a vuvuzela before."

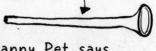

"There's a good reason for that," Mum says. Uncle Kevin is encouraging me to try it out.

"Go on, Tom, give it a good **BLAST!**"

"You're loving this, aren't you?"
Dad says to him.

"Hey, boys – if you want, I'll buy you your own vuvuzelas so you can have one too," Dad tells the cousins, which seems to PERK them up a bit.

Then I have a go at BLOWING it.

I try my best and make a kind of **BLAAAAH** sound.

"Keep practising, Tom," Granny Pet tells me.

"Can he practise round at yours?"
Mum wants to know.

"Of course – he's our grandson, after all. It's just SO nice seeing you all again!" Granny Pet smiles and gives me and the cousins a BIG HUG.

I have another go at trying to make it sound less like a DUCK.

BLAHHH BLAHHHHH BLAAAAAAAH

Which works. "I'm going to use this at my next BAND practice!" I announce.

"That's what we thought," Granddad Joe says.

"In the meantime I can look after it safely in the shed," Dad tells me.

I'm not falling for that old trick again.

"No, it's FINE, Dad – I'll keep it with me," I say. Then the cousins have a go too.

BLAHHHHHHHH

BLaHHHhHHHh

We have a competition to see who can make the LOUDEST NOISE, until Mum shouts, "YOU all WIN' – that's enough vuvuzela for today, PLEASE!"

I do a couple more **BLLaAHHsSS**, just because I can.

Granny Pet disappears upstairs to tell Delia about the FAMILY outing. And when she comes back down, she looks VERY happy, which is a SURPRISE.

"What a LOVELY young lady Delia is," she says. Mum and Dad look CONFUSED as **THAT** doesn't sound like Delia at ALL.

"Are you SURE it was DELIA you were talking to?" I ask, just in case.

"Yes, Tom. Delia is going to come with us on our trip to **Crambly Castle**. She says she's looking FORWARD to it."

(We all do another HUH? like we can't quite believe it.)

"Well done, Mum! I don't know WHAT you said to her, but it's great she's coming," my mum says. Then she calls Granny Pet the "Teenager Whisperer" (whatever that is).

I'm VERY surprised Delia said YES. Maybe ALIENS took her away and replaced her with someone nicer instead?

Repeat after me: "I love everything."

I love everything!

It's the ONLY answer.

Having a vuvuzela ALMOST makes up for missing out on the BIG BISCUITS (but not quite).

So I'm SUPER HAPPY when Granny Mavis tells me she's found some MORE.

Thanks, Granny!

Uncle Kevin, Aunty Alice and the cousins are
about to leave, so I GRAB a biscuit and shove it
in my mouth so there's NO chance of
Mum asking me to SHARE or anything
silly like that.

Uncle Kevin says he's sorry again that they can't
come with us. "I'll be sorting out football kit
while you're all having an EPIC time."

 "If you say so, Kevin,"
Dad adds.

Then Aunty Alice wants to know if Granny Mavis

 has a special recipe for the
EXTRA-LARGE BISCUITS.
"The boys love them, so I might try making a few."

Granny Mavis says, "It's VERY simple – you just
mix all the biscuit ingredients together,
add a LOT of ...

... LEFTOVERS and whizz them up in a blender. I don't like to be wasteful and it makes **bigger biscuits** too!"

(I stop eating.)

"Did Mavis just say 'leftovers'?" Aunty Alice whispers.

"She did," Mum says. "Best not to find out the details," she adds.

The Wrinklies don't seem that bothered.

Bug kebab

Yum.

"We've eaten all kinds of things on our travels," they remind us.

I'm trying NOT to think about what LEFTOVERS Granny might have used.

It almost puts me OFF my biscuit ...

... but not quite.

(They still taste nice and that's the main thing.)

After everyone's gone Mum goes to write the
FAMILY OUTING on to the calendar,
but Granny Pet has already done it.
Then she notices something else.
"Tom, your TROPICAL **disco**
is on the SAME day as our family outing.
It doesn't start until 5.30, so you should be OK."

"I WAFFF to be," I say, finishing off the
last bit of biscuit.
Now I have **TWO** (hopefully exciting)
things to look forward to. ☺

Delia ventures downstairs now everyone's left.
So I ask her, "Are you ACTUALLY coming with us?"

"Don't sound SO surprised. I want to spend
quality time with my little brother."

"Seriously?" (I'm shocked.)

"**NO**... I really like Joe and Pet, and they asked me to come, so what's the problem?"

"Did they give you a present?" I wonder.

"Pet gave me a biscuit. It was **enormous**, too."

"And did you eat it?" I check.

 "Why? You're not getting it – I've eaten it already. Bad luck, Tom."

"Oh, no reason. Granny was just telling us about her SPECIAL biscuit ingredients, that's all."

(I'll save the LEFTOVERS as a surprise for another day.)

In the meantime I treat Delia to a **bLAST** of my vuvuzela...

Arghhh

BLAAAAAH

Which she enjoys.

In the morning my HAIR is being awkward again. It takes me AGES to get ready for school because it WON'T stay out of my eyes.

Mum's hidden her hair gel so I can't even use that now. I do the best I can to push it out of my face then head downstairs, where Delia is being her jolly self. Every time I *LEAN* forward to eat some cereal, my hair drops in a way that makes it hard to eat.

"TOM, your HAIR is dangling in your bowl – that's disgusting."

I try *FLICKING* the hair out of my face, but manage to spill some cereal and send a few cornflakes FLYING in Delia's direction.

Cornflake

"What are you DOING?" she shouts at me.

"Sharing my breakfast with you," I say,

while rescuing my cereal before it all spills.

As soon as Mum and Dad join us they start talking about my hair as well.

 "It's getting far too **long**, Tom – it'll need a cut soon," Mum tells me.

"He's just been *FLICKING* it in his food too. It's gross," Delia adds.

"Can I eat my BREAKFAST, please?" I say, like nothing's WRONG at all.

Then Dad says, "Speaking of hair – not that I have any – but Granddad Joe's hair has GROWN a lot more as he's got older. It's much THICKER, too."

 Mum agrees. "They both look a LOT younger, don't you think?"

"If I wore a *'syrup'* like Joe, I'd look younger too," Dad points out.

"**F**rank! Are you sure that's what it is?"

Mum sounds surprised.

"WHAT are you talking about?"

"Don't worry about it," Mum tells me, which makes me more curious. Dad said ⌐syrup⌐ and that's confusing because IF *syrup* makes you look YOUNGER, then everyone (including me) should put LOADS on their pancakes.

"He might even have more than one *syrup* for different occasions!" Dad adds.

(Now I'm REALLY confused.)

"Does Granddad like *syrup* a LOT?"

"They're talking about his HAIR!"

Mum looks at Dad and says, "It's your fault - you'd better explain what you mean."

"It's called Cockney rhyming slang*. *Syrup*
is short for '*syrup* OF FIGS', which
rhymes with WIG."

(I'm still confused.)

"It's OBVIOUS he's got a WIG," Delia says.

GRANDDAD JOE has a WIG!
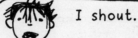
I shout.

"DON'T you say a WORD, Tom! He probably
doesn't want us to know about it."

"He should get a better WIG then,"
Dad mutters.

"So THAT'S why he didn't want to do
THIS," I say, and I RUB my head while
patting my stomach. "It all makes sense now."

Delia gets up to leave. "You must be SO proud of
him," she says to Mum and Dad, while looking at me.
It sounds like she's being nice – but I'm not sure.

* For more Cockney rhyming slang see page 227

"Come on, Tom, off to school. We'll talk about your haircut later," says Mum.

"Dad needs a haircut too – and his will be quicker!" I say before I leave.

"Very FUNNY, Tom."
(I think so. :))
Hair

Outside it's really windy, and Derek is squinting as he waits for me. "The wind's blowing DUST in my EYES," he tells me and squints some more.

My hair is FLYING all over the place too.

Derek opens his eyes just enough to tell me I've got a cornflake in my hair.

I take it out as we start walking.

"I've nearly finished my LATEST **SPY BOOK**," he says and takes it out of his bag to show me.

"You can borrow it after me if you want."

Looking at the title, I understand why Derek is so SUSPICIOUS of The Wrinklies.

I check my watch and see we have EXACTLY ten minutes to get to school.

"Do you know what a *syrup* is?" I ask Derek as we keep walking.

"Well, it's sticky stuff you put on pancakes, OR it's Cockney rhyming slang for WIG: *syrup* of figs - WIG."

"Oh... How do you know that?"

"My dad told me.
We've got a book on it too."
(I need to see this book.)

I tell Derek about Granddad Joe's 'syrup'.
HE suggests that the next time we go to see
The Wrinklies we should look for any SPY
evidence.

 (Good idea...) When we get to school

the wind has been SO

BLOWY that Mr Keen, who's at the gate, says,

 "Who's that hiding under that HAIR?"

"It's me, sir - Tom Gates."

"So it is," he says, and Derek LAUGHS.

When I get to class, AMY tells me I've got a

LEAF in my hair (which is embarrassing).

 Then Marcus tells me

I look like a ZOMBIE.

"Your hair's all wild too."

"It's not THAT bad," I say.

"It is..." Marcus adds.

"This is you, Tom..."

Grrrrrrrrrr

Marcus gets UP and starts SHUFFLING round his desk and making weird noises like a ZOMBIE.

I admit it's quite a good **zombie** walk, but Mr Fullerman still tells him to sit down. Marcus DRAGS his foot all the way back to his chair.

"It's because of your crazy hair," he whispers.

"Thanks, Marcus," I say.

There's a reminder about the TROPICAL disco on the board. I start telling AMY all about my family outing and how it's on the same DAY as the **disco**.

"I thought we were going to Disneyland, but it's only **Crambly Castle**. I have to get back in time for the **disc**, though. I'll use my **WATCH** alarm." **AMY** doesn't seem that bothered about my problem.

Marcus, on the other hand, tells me I could go as a

"I could ... if I was really stupid," I sigh.
Then, weirdly, I start to hear **BUZZING** in my hair. So I give my head a REALLY good SHAKE, but it's still there.

I SHAKE some more and this time a FLY →  drops out of my hair and on to the desk. It sits there for a second and then FLIES off.

Marcus starts shouting,

"FLY ALERT!
FLY ALERT!"

"Did that fly just drop out of your hair, Tom?"
AMY asks.

"I think so. It was VERY windy outside. LEAVES, flies - what can you do?"

NEWS travels ~~ex~~ *fast* in Oakfield School. Especially FLY NEWS.

Derek finds me at break time and says, "Did a fly drop out of your hair?"

"Sort of ... I shook it out and it landed on my desk and flew off. It was only TINY. It's not like I've got NITS or anything!" I tell him just as

AMY and her friends walk past.

"I DON'T have nits," I say again.

"Just FLIES," Derek adds helpfully.

"ONE fly," I correct him.

"Thanks for that, Derek."
Before we go back into class I ask him to do me a
FAVOUR.

"Will you check there's nothing else hiding in my
hair? Just in case..."

"OK," Derek agrees, while trying
not to LAUGH.

He has a quick look and tells me it's all fine, just
as AMY and her friends walk back past us again.

"Nothing to see here," I say,
             but inside I'm CRINGING.

       (Maybe it's time to get a haircut after all.)

At the end of the school day, the LAST thing I'm expecting to see by the gates is Mum and BOTH my grannies all WAVING at me.

"Cooee, Tom!"

"TOM!"

"You're popular!" Derek says.

"I don't know why they're here," I manage to tell him before Granny Mavis moves in for a BIG HUG, followed closely by Granny Pet.

"Isn't this nice? We're taking you with us," Mum says.

"Where?" I manage to ask.

"To the HAIRDRESSER'S! We're all booked in for haircuts TOGETHER." HUH?

"Which hairdresser's?"

"Have a great time!" Derek says as he waves BYE. AMY, Florence and Indrani are all watching my grannies FUSS over me.

"Aren't you going to introduce me to your friends, Tom?" Granny Pet wants to know.

(Really?)

"Oh... This is AMY, Florence and Indrani," I say.

"Hello," they reply.

"We're taking Tom to the hairdresser's," Mum explains.

(They don't need to <u>know</u> that.)

For some reason, AMY announces "Tom had a FLY in his hair today, didn't you?"

"It wasn't there for very long..." I say and head off in what turns out to be the wrong direction.

"THIS WAY, TOM!"

"Coming..."

"We've booked a nice CUT and BLOW DRY for you. OR you can have a PERM, like me!" Granny Mavis says.

(I think she's JOKING.)

"I don't want a PERM,"

I tell her, just in case she means it.

"I had a perm once - it didn't go well," Mum remembers.

As we're walking, I have a feeling I know where we're going, and then we STOP right outside...

(Uh-oh.)

HAIRTASTIC

We go in and I try not to look anyone in the EYE, but Granny Pet keeps introducing me to everyone.

"This is our grandson - isn't he LOVELY!"

I don't mind <u>too</u> much once I'm offered a drink and my own small packet of vanilla WAFERS.

"Excellent!" I say and smile.

I start to wonder how they're going to cut my hair, because looking around I can't see ANYONE else who looks like ME having their hair done.

AT ALL.

I'm shown to a seat between both my grannies and I have to put on a swirly cape thing. I'm about to tell the nice lady who's cutting my hair what I want when Mum comes over and does it for me.

"Neater, shorter, and the same style – is that OK, Tom?"

Which is about right.

$\mathbb{I}$ have my hair washed and then I go back to my seat by the window where the grannies are having a CHAT.

"Look at us all matching!" Granny Mavis says. (So we are.)

The hairdresser clips up my hair and starts cutting it. I sit back and open my wafers while looking at a magazine about GARDENS, which is not that interesting. Instead I concentrate on nibbling my wafer in sections so it lasts longer.

Vanilla wafer →

Break off the layers

It's a complicated process, and I'm SO engrossed in how many layers of wafer there are that I don't hear the tap on the window until the hairdresser says,

"Is that a friend of yours?"

Oh no.

"Sort of," I say and try to hide behind the magazine.

It's Marcus Meldrew, who's grinning at me through the window. (Brilliant.) He's pulling faces and being silly. I pretend to be REALLY INTERESTED in the magazine until he gets the message and STOPS – which takes a lot longer than I expect.

Eventually he gets bored and leaves me alone.

I haven't really been taking much notice of what's happening to my hair until the hairdresser says,

"There. ALL done."

She holds up a mirror so I
can see the BACK of my head.

"WHERE'S MY HAIR GONE?"

It is the same style, but LOADS shorter.

Both my grannies and Mum say it looks great, but
I'm not so sure.

"I'm practically **BALD,**" I tell them.

Mum says I'm EXAGGERATING, and the
hairdresser wants to take a photo of me because
she thinks my haircut is FIERCE!

"Really?" I say. (I think that's a good thing.)

I let her take a few snaps after I've
removed the *swirly gown.*

At least I can see properly now,

I suppose.

But it still feels a bit weird,

not having hair.

Mum and I go and sit in the waiting area as the grannies aren't finished yet. Then the lady who told me and Derek to "MOVE ON" walks past, but thanks to my haircut, I don't think she recognizes me.

So that's something.

I manage to avoid being seen until Dad comes to pick us up.

"WOW! Look at your amazing haircuts. You ladies look like FILM STARS!"

"Don't we!" Mum agrees.

"That's very short, Tom," is all he can say about mine, followed by, "It will grow."

"Thanks, Dad," I sigh. (It will.)

By the time we get home, I've almost got used to my short hair, and I do like being able to SEE.

Unfortunately ... Delia is the first person I bump into.

"**WHAT** did you do to upset the hairdresser, Tom?" she asks me.

"Nothing. I've just got short hair, that's all."

"**Y**ou really have," Delia agrees. Then, because I **know** what she's like, I do an excellent SWERVE out of the way to avoid a PAT on the head.

"Way too slow!"

I LAUGH.

Then I go to my room and use my **SECRET AGENT PEN** to draw some excellent pictures of Delia with a few NEW hairstyles – which she will NEVER SEE!

Ha! Ha! HA!

In the morning my HAIR takes up a lot less TIME, which is good news as I get to have two bowls of cereal before ANYONE comes downstairs.

(Result!)

I've brought my drawing of Delia with me as it's fun to *WAFT* it under her nose.

"Look, I've done a lovely picture of you," I tell her.

"There's nothing on it," she says.

"Oh, but there is!" I put it in my bag so I can show Derek later. With my EXTRA time I decide to take my vuvuzela into school with me. I put it behind my back, but I'm so busy AVOIDING Mum that I don't spot Dad, who says,

"Hands up anyone who's trying to sneak a vuvuzela into school?"

(I say nothing.)

Dad takes it from me and says, "That'll be you, then. You can't take it to school – I'll look after it for you."

"Do you promise? You won't take it to a charity shop, will you?"

Mum hears me and LAUGHS because that's happened before. 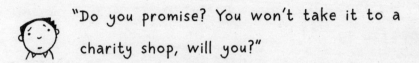 Ha! Ha!

"Of course we won't," Dad says and then follows me out of the house, where Derek is waiting.

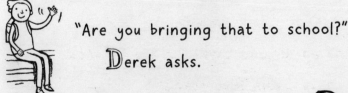

"Are you bringing that to school?" Derek asks.

"No, Dad's looking after it for me," I sigh. Then, for some reason, Dad decides to **BLOW** into the vuvuzela ...

REALLY LOUDLY ...

BLAHH HHAAa

just as June's dad walks past — which is a
SURPRISE for **ALL** of us.
Watching Dad apologize is FUN.

"Nice hair, Tom," Derek says.

"THANKS!"

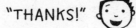 "It's very short..."

"Nowhere for flies to hide!"

I say, which is true.

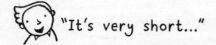

M**r** K**een** <u>STILL</u> doesn't recognize me when I
get to school. "Morning, Derek ... and
who's this? TOM, is
that YOU?!"

"Yes, sir - it's me."

If walking into class is anything to go by, I'm
going to get LOTS more comments ALL DAY.
Mark Clump just shouts,

HAIRCUT!

at me and nothing else. As we walk past the
TR🍍PICAL **disc🔮** poster, **Buster Jones**
says, 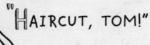 GATESY! Where's your hair?

I point to my head. "Still there!" Just.
Marcus joins in too.

"HAIRCUT, TOM!"

"You don't miss a thing,
do you, Marcus..."

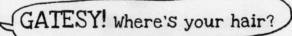

141

I FORGOT that I have my SPY WATCH in my bag. NOW seems like a very good time to put it on and find the **raspberry** sound effect.

Rrraassspp
Rasssppp

I press it every time Marcus says something silly about my hair, which is a LOT.

You hair's shrunk.

Rrraaassspp

Then I accidentally press it when Mr Fullerman starts TALKING to the class.

Morning, Class 5F. I'll be coming round to pick up your homework, so if you could get it ready to hand to me...

Rrraaasssppp

My timing isn't great, which Marcus enjoys. I'm not **LAUGHING**, because I don't have any homework to hand in.

Ha! Ha!

Uh-oh... I'm not sure HOW this happened, but I need to think of something *SUPER FAST.* I get out my workbook and STARE at the empty page ... which gives me an **IDEA.**

So I quickly write this...

Mr Fullerman,

I <u>have</u> done my homework. The trouble is, I wrote the WHOLE THING (accidentally) with my **SECRET AGENT PEN**, which has invisible ink.

It's really *good* ...

... you just can't see it.

SORRY.

 MY HOMEWORK ☺

I hand in my homework and hope it will be a while before Mr Fullerman looks at mine.

Phew.

That's done the trick (for now).

AMY has done her homework (obviously). She asks me if I'm going to come to **CRAFT CLASS** at lunchtime.

"Lunchtime? I don't think so," I say.

"We're helping to make props and paint scenery for the TROPICAL **disco**.

You'd like that," she says.

"**YES!** I'll be there!"

(I've changed my mind.)

"I'm going too," Marcus says, which still doesn't put me off.

"Nice hair, Tom," AMY tells me.

"Thanks – it's short, though," I say.

"It'll grow back," AMY says.

"In ten years' time..." Marcus tells me, so I look for my watch to make another **raspberry** noise.

"Listen to this," I tell AMY.

Uh-oh...

You're in trouble!

MOOOOOO!
MOOOOOOOO!
MOOOOOO!

I can't get it to STOP **MOOING!**

OK, Tom. Bring your watch here. You can have it back at the end of the day.

Mr Fullerman confiscates my watch.

(Groan.)

Not only do I HAVE to give him my WATCH, but when I come back from break, Mr Fullerman tells me I have to go to **study club** at lunchtime as well! 😞 My **SECRET AGENT PEN** excuse didn't work, so I'm missing out on **CRAFT CLASS** and all the TR🍍PICAL **disc🪩** painting, which is <u>very</u> annoying.

Mr Fullerman doesn't want me to fall behind. **"It shouldn't take you long, Tom,"** he says. **"Especially as you've already done your invisible homework. You can just remember it and write it out again. Good haircut, too."**

I have lunch quickly, then try to do my work *SUPER FAST* so I can try and get to **CRAFT CLASS.** (That's my PLAN.) I'm listening to some kids practise for a spelling test, and then I hear something else...

GATESY! HAIRCUT!

I wave at **Buster** and smile while I try and THINK of a story. Nothing has really worked out for me today. I have been VERY unlucky.

PING!

Then I get a good story idea.

The Unlucky Boy

By Tom Gates

Once upon a time there was a boy who was a really FANTASTIC person, but VERY unlucky.

It wasn't HIS fault that he used the wrong pen to do his homework. ⚬ ➤ He picked up a **SECRET AGENT PEN** by ACCIDENT, and the words he wrote only went and disappeared after he'd spent TEN HOURS writing them.

How UNLUCKY is THAT? (Very.)

Then he went to get his hair cut and the hairdresser got carried away going SNIP SNIP SNIP

... and before you could say "HAIRCUT" ➤

... most of his hair had disappeared. When he went into school the boy who sat next to him wouldn't STOP going on about it. "HAIRCUT! HAIRCUT!" he kept saying, which is almost as annoying as the boy's next-door NEIGHBOUR, who liked to SING very bad songs that kept the unlucky boy awake. It was VERY hard to concentrate in the spelling test, so the unlucky boy didn't get the result he'd HOPED for. Then the boy's teacher sent him to **study club,** where the boy wrote a spectacular piece of homework that was SO brilliant it got lots of MERITS and that meant he wasn't unlucky any more. THE END.

YES! ALL done. I might still make it to the

CRAFT CLUB. I'm about to leave when **Buster** calls

me over.

 "I'm going to be late, **Buster.** I need to go!"

But **Buster** keeps calling me <u>over</u>.

"GATESY!"

"Did you see what I drew on the

disco poster?"

"I did - it was FUNNY."

"Did you see the face of Mr Keeno?"

he wants to know.

"Yes, it was very good."

"Mr Keen saw it too, that's why I'm HERE," he says.

"Bad luck **Buster**," I sympathize.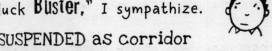

"I've been SUSPENDED as corridor

monitor for now."

"You'll get it back, **Buster.** You're good at keeping

kids moving. See you later!" I know he wants a

chat but I have to get to the **CRAFT CLUB.** ☺

I've MISSED CRAFT CLUB.

 Awwwwwww

Everyone's leaving and going back to class.

 "WHERE were you?" **AMY** asks.

"**Study club**," I say.

"**CRAFT CLUB** was great. We painted a BEACH as a backdrop for photos and we made paper palm trees* and all kinds of other things too," she tells me excitedly.

 "Sounds great..." I sigh.

"**LOOK** at the PAPER palm tree I made, Tom! How was **study club?**" Marcus asks (like he really wants to know).

 "Great, thanks..."

* See how to make a paper palm tree on page 228-229

"The TROPICAL **disco** is going to be SOOOOOO GOOD."

Marcus is super annoying.

Even **Mr Fullerman** comes in wearing a

❀**FLOWER**❀ GARLAND.

"Just getting into the TROPICAL **disco** mood!"

he tells us.

"I hope you're **ALL** going to dress up in your best tropical outfits!"

He smiles. It seems like the WHOLE CLASS CHEERS and AMY and Marcus WAVE their paper palm trees in the air. I don't have one, so I just say "YEAH" with as much enthusiasm as I can - then I hand in my homework.

YEAH...

_HOORAY!

I manage to get over the disappointment of missing out on the TR🍍PICAL **disc**🪩 stuff fairly quickly. Doing a TR🍍PICAL doodle helps, as does thinking about my visit to The Wrinklies after school today.

(My tropical name)

When Granny Pet said, "Pop by any time!" I'm not sure they were expecting to see me quite so often.

They've met quite a few of my friends already. I've brought Norman and Solid round, and Derek's coming with me today. He's written a list of **SPY THINGS** we should be looking out for, though I'm not expecting to find much. (Maybe a wig or two, if Dad's right!)

Here's Derek's LIST:

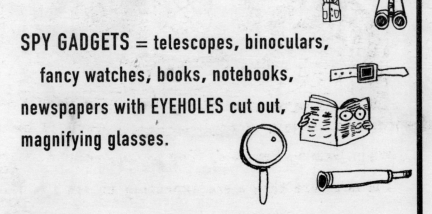

SPY STUFF TO LOOK OUT FOR

DISGUISES = wigs, glasses,
fake beards, moustaches, HATS,
long coats with high collars.

SPY GADGETS = telescopes, binoculars,
fancy watches, books, notebooks,
newspapers with EYEHOLES cut out,
magnifying glasses.

I remember to get my watch back from **Mr Fullerman** at the end of the day.

No mooing in class.

Then **Derek** and I go home first as Rooster is coming with us to see **The Wrinklies.**

"He needs a walk," **Derek** tells me.

We get to their flat and ring the bell. "Look out for anything suspicious!" he whispers.

Then Granny Pet and Granddad Joe open the door.

Hi.

"You've caught us MID beauty routine! We can wash our face packs off in a few minutes."

Derek nudges me. "THAT's suspicious."

When we get inside, **Derek** nudges me AGAIN. "Look over there!"

"**HATS!** Who has that many hats?" he asks.

"My grandparents?" I say.

Derek gets out his LIST and ticks off HATS. ✓ "Hmmmmm..."

The Wrinklies come in with FRESH, CLEAN faces and Granddad Joe pets Rooster as he sniffs around their flat. "I see you've got your watch on, Tom!" he notices.

"I LOVE IT. It's got loads of really good SOUNDS on it, INCLUDING THIS ONE!"

I press the DOG BARKING sound, which sends Rooster **CRAZY!** WOOF WOOF WOOF WOOF

He runs off into the corridor.

"Don't worry, he'll be fine. Let him look round," Granny Pet tells Derek.

"Have you figured out ALL the other things your watch does, Tom?" Granddad Joe asks. Then he shows me the SUPER-BRIGHT torch and a button that records messages too.

Wow! Who knew?

"I've got a watch like that, only mine has MORE GADGETS on it," Granddad says, which has Derek whispering, "See? See?"

"It's just a watch!" I say as we follow them into the kitchen to have something to eat.
Granny Pet asks Derek all kinds of questions about his hobbies, his parents, and his dad's record collection.

"He has a LOT of bands I've never heard of,"
Derek explains while eating a sandwich.
The Wrinklies want to know
what bands we like, which is
an easy question.

→ **DUDE3**   **DUDE3**

we both say straight away.

"Ooh, I've not heard of them. Can you dance to
their music? We LOVE a dance, don't we, Joe?"
Before I can answer, The Wrinklies are both
up and dancing, which is alarming and unexpected.

WOW...

(Especially for Derek.)
We're still watching
them do their crazy dancing when ROOSTER
comes running back into the room ...

... WEARING A **WIG!**

It's like he's found a friend.

Grrrrr

"ROOSTER, put the furry thing down!" Derek shouts.

"Don't worry, I have others!" Granddad Joe says, which is just as well.

Derek apologizes for Rooster and thinks we should go. "I don't want him to do anything else," he tells me.

While Derek's trying to wrestle the wig away from Rooster, Granny Pet ignores them both and asks me if I'm looking forward to our TRIP at the weekend.

"Yes, I am. **Crambly Castle's** going to be great," I tell them while Rooster is still growling.

The Wrinklies let Rooster keep the **WIG,** which he seems **VERY HAPPY** about.

He's not letting go.

They also give me an envelope. "These are your tickets for **Crambly Castle.** Give them to your Mum and Dad, OK?" I nod and put them safely in my pocket.

"Your grandparents are FUNNY!"

Derek says on the way home.

"So they're not SPIES, then?" I say.

"Maybe," he replies. (They're not.)

Back at home, Mum and Dad aren't surprised when

I tell them about the WIGS.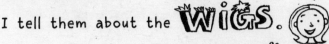

"I wish I'd seen that!"  Dad LAUGHS.

"So are they all set for Saturday?"

Mum asks me, trying to be serious.

"The wigs are," Dad jokes, and Mum gives him

a LOOK. 👁👁

"PLEASE don't go on about the wigs, you two."

"What wigs?"

Delia wants to know.

"You'll see on Saturday, IF you're still coming?"

I ask, because she usually changes her mind.

"I'm still coming. I know you'd miss me otherwise,"

Delia says.

Then I remember about the ▭ envelope, so I pass it to Mum. "See? I don't forget EVERYTHING. It's our tickets to **Crambly Castle.**"

"Excellent - we'll bring a picnic, too!"
I take the opportunity to remind Mum and Dad how IMPORTANT it is that I don't miss the TROPICAL **disco**.

"**W**e will be back for it, won't we?"

  "I don't see why not," Dad says.

"We'll be FINE. There's plenty of time," Mum adds.

 "I'm travelling with Joe and Pet, so you don't have to worry about me," Delia says.

Mum and Dad seem surprised that Delia is so keen. "OK," they both say together.

"Just so you know, I'm not worried about you," I tell Delia.

Delia <u>not</u> being in the car means **TONS** more space for **ME**, which I'm very pleased about.

"We haven't been on a TRIP like this for a **LONG** time, have we?" Mum says. Dad makes a "Hmmmmmmm..." noise.

"We could make going on trips TOGETHER a REGULAR thing!" Mum says, which sounds like a good idea to me.

Delia is the voice of **GLOOM** and says, "Don't get carried away - it's <u>OUR</u> family you're talking about. I mean, a FAMILY TRIP with us lot. What could possibly go wrong?"

After listening to Delia, I go upstairs and make sure I have EVERYTHING READY for the TROPICAL **disco**, because I really don't want ANYTHING to go wrong.

I have my ticket and my SUNSHINE T-shirt. It's the most tropical thing I have to wear. I'd love to take the vuvuzela with me, but it's too big. (Next time.)

I set my watch to go off TWICE: once to wake me up, then again at 16:00 – an <u>HOUR</u> before the **disco** starts so I'm not late.

This is unusually organized for me, but I actually quite like it. As I'm checking that I've got everything, Derek attracts my attention from his window.

He's got Rooster with him ...

... who's still wearing the **WIG**.

I write two signs about tomorrow

and hold them up.

SEE YOU at
the TROPICAL
DISCO!

It's going
to be
EPIC

(I hope so.)

Yes!

Beep beep! Beep beep! BEEP!

I'm up like a ══ FLASH and I

get dressed really fast as well. Amazingly,

Delia is already AWAKE and having her breakfast.

I'm immediately suspicious that

she's UP to something.

"Are you STILL coming

with us?" I ask.

"Of course - but I'm going with Joe and Pet in

their hire car so we can chat."

(So far so good.)

Mum and Dad have been organized (like me) and got a bag ready for the day. Just for **FUN** I leave my vuvuzela next to it like I'm bringing it with us. Ha! Ha! (That will worry them.)

I have my breakfast and don't argue with Delia much – just about how much cereal <u>she's</u> taken. I check that I have my **disco** tickets and **SECRET AGENT PEN** in my pocket, and that my WATCH is set up.

I'm ready nice and EARLY, which gives me some time to have a go at making a paper palm tree. I manage to make TWO by the time The Wrinklies arrive. They're easier to make than I thought.

(It's already 10:30 .)

Granddad Joe is wearing a HAT, so checking out his WIG is going to be harder today (which is probably a good thing). Dad comes to tell us that he's had a call from Granny Mavis.

"Bob's only gone and SNAPPED his false teeth in half biting on a TOFFEE!"

"Sounds like something Bob would do!" Mum says.

"Mavis is taking him to the emergency dentist to see if they can fix them – they have an appointment later today. What a SHAME they can't come," Dad says.

"I bet Mavis was cross!"

"Mavis is more cross about Bob telling everyone that he broke his teeth on one of her BISCUITS!"

I can imagine Granddad saying that.

Ha! Ha!

Delia tells Joe and Pet, "I'll wait in
the car for you."

"Fine, we'll see you there. Here's your
ticket." Mum tries to give Delia a quick hug,
but she ducks out of the way.

"The tickets are for 11:30, so we've
got plenty of time to get there.
You can follow us if you like?" Granddad Joe asks.

"Don't worry, we know where we're going. I'm
driving so we won't get lost," Mum
tells him.
"If I was driving we wouldn't get
lost either," Dad says.
"If you say so," Mum replies.
I don't care WHO drives just so long as we're not
LATE back.
Then The Wrinklies both say - "Come and have a
look at the car we've hired - it's a lovely ...

... **SMART** little runaround."

"Can I go with <u>THEM</u> instead?" I ask, as their car is <u>SO</u> much nicer than ours.

"**No**, Tom. You're staying with **US**," Mum tells me straight away. Dad's speechless.
The Wrinklies say I can come <u>back</u> with them, and I won't even mind squashing in next to Delia, who's waving at me while looking **SMUG** and comfortable.

When they drive off, the car sort of **GLIDES** past us.

"See you there!" Granny Pet shouts.

"That car even SOUNDS better than ours,"
I point out.

"Yes, but we OWN our car — theirs is
just rented for the day," Mum explains.

"We don't own it YET," Dad says.

"Besides, it doesn't matter what type of car you
have so long as it gets from A to B.
Isn't that right, Frank?"

"Yes, I suppose so," Dad agrees.

Before we set off, I tell them what the time is.
"It's 10:45. We have until 11:30 to get to
Crambly Castle and we have to leave
at FOUR if I don't want to MISS
the disco." I show Mum and Dad
my watch just to make sure they know.

Just
saying...

"Thanks, Tom, that's VERY helpful,"
Dad sort of agrees.

"Isn't this fun?" Mum smiles.

The Wrinklies' car is in front of us and we follow it for a while.

"Can you see them? I can't," Mum asks Dad.

"Just keep going – there'll be a sign soon," Dad says.

"Do you know the way, then?" Mum checks.

"**YES** – don't worry, we'll be fine," Dad tells us, right before we get **STUCK** in a really

BAD TRAFFIC JAM.

Sigh

We hardly move at all for AGES. Every five minutes I let Mum and Dad know the time – which I think is helpful.

"It's 11:05 now."

"Ok, Tom. There's no need for the time checks." Dad sounds tense.

Then Delia rings up and says they're already at the **castle!** "That was quick - we're **still** going really slowly," Mum sighs, as we MISS the RIGHT turn and have to take the NEXT one.

Dad tells Delia on the phone not to wait for us.
"Go into the **castle** because we could be a while."

(I hope not.)

"I thought YOU knew the way!"
(Now <u>Mum</u> sounds tense.)

"I do ... and we're going the right way NOW."
Mum and Dad are both getting annoyed, so I make a joke to cheer them up.
"Who wants to hear me play the vuvuzela?"

"NO!" they SHOUT really quickly.

  "I don't have it, really.
It's 11:20 ."
Just so they know.

We get to the **castle** at ▮12:00▮ and drive up a long gravel path to the car park.

 "This brings back memories," Mum tells us.

"LOOK, THERE'S THE **castle!**" I shout.

"And there's Joe and Pet's car," Dad points out. "Let's park next to them."

"Or we could park closer to the entrance," Mum suggests, but there aren't any spaces, so we drive around the whole car park again. "Don't say a word," Mum tells Dad as she parks in the space he pointed at before.

"I'm just glad we're here."

"ME TOO! And it's not long until my TR🍍PICAL **disc🪩!**" I remind them in case they've forgotten.

Dad takes the picnic bag and gets a ticket for the car park. "That was expensive!" he says as he puts the ticket in the window.

At the **castle** entrance a man stops us from going in. "We have tickets already," Mum tells him and hands them over.

"Sorry, you're too LATE — these tickets are for the 11:30 slot. You'll have to buy new ones."

You're kidding! Dad says.

"No, sir, I'm not kidding."

"Come on, you're not exactly BUSY!" Mum points out, trying not to get cross.

"No ticket, no entrance."

When Dad finds out how much the new tickets are he's not happy. "HOW MUCH? We only want to SEE the **castle**, not BUY IT!"

"Well, sir, it costs a lot to run a place of such historical importance."

It's not the best time for me to tell Mum, "I'm hungry," but I can't help it.

"It's OK, Tom, we have our picnic. Let's just go in, shall we?"

"Sorry, no picnics on the protected land. We do have a cafe, or you can eat in the car park over there."
He points out a sad bench.

I think Mum and Dad are going to EXPLODE.

AND I'm still hungry.

"FINE!" Dad manages to say. We take

the picnic bag back to the car and Dad

stuffs drinks and crisps into his pocket

and puts a wafer under his hat.

"Shhhh! Don't say a word," he whispers.

Mum tries to phone Delia but can't get a signal.

"They're in there somewhere – we'll catch up with

them," she says. Once we're out of sight of the

man at the gate, Dad gives me the wafer,

which has melted a bit, but it keeps me going.

"You could have got me one as well!"

Mum points out.

"It's a small hat – sorry."

We can't go into the **castle** until I've finished

**NO FOOD
OR DRINK**

my wafer, which doesn't take long. The first

thing we see is some armour. Dad and I stand

next to it while Mum takes a photo.

Straight away someone tells us off.

"STAND BACK FROM THE ARMOUR!"

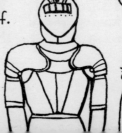

You're too close.

(179)

"NOT so close to the exhibits, thank you!"

"Sorry!" Mum mutters and we all move on.

"This is fun, isn't it?" she whispers.

Sort of... I say.

We walk round the **castle** and through

lots of DARK ROOMS that are quite cold

and have STERN-looking paintings on the walls.

There's a sign to the TOWER,
which looks interesting.
"We might see the others
from up there," I suggest,
because I want to go up to
the top. We get to the stairs and there's another
sign that says:

"Oh, well – let's go to the
dungeon instead, it's not far,"
Mum suggests.

Closed for
RESTORATION.

I check my watch and it's already 12:45.
(No wonder I'm HUNGRY.) We follow the signs and
the SAME MAN from the gate is sitting there –
looking **official.**

Hello again, he says.

"We're going to the **dungeon!**"
I tell him as we try to go down the stairs.

"Not with these tickets, I'm afraid. The **dungeon** isn't
included. You'll have to buy an extra ticket outside."

"That's RIDICULOUS! Why didn't you tell us?"
Mum wants to know.

"You didn't ask. I am sorry."

"Come on, shall we get something to eat instead?"
Mum suggests.

I say, Finally! because who wants to see the
dungeon anyway? (I do, but I'm also very hungry...)

Mum tries to call Delia again, but there's still no signal. We leave the inside of the **castle** and head out to the courtyard. Mum looks at a MAP to find the cafe. "I wonder where they are?" she says.

I check the time. IT'S

13:00.

(Officially lunchtime!)

Dad takes us in one direction, then turns around again. "It's THIS WAY! The signs aren't very clear," he says.

I remind them again that I'm

"REALLY HUNGRY!"

"OK, Tom. The cafe's over there and the **castle's** empty, so it should be quiet," Mum tells me.

Only it's **NOT** - there's a long QUEUE.

"Let's not wait around. Shall we come back

in a while?" Dad suggests.

"But I'M HUNGRY, THOUGH!" I say again.

"I've got some crisps, Tom. You can have those."

"OK," I agree. "What flavour are they?"

"Crisp flavour," Dad tells me.

Then for some reason he decides to put his head in

the stocks for **FUN**. He opens it up and slips his

hands in as well while I put my feet in the other one.

"Now THAT'S a good PHOTO!" Mum LAUGHS

and gets out her phone to take a picture.

"Don't move," she says...

(183)

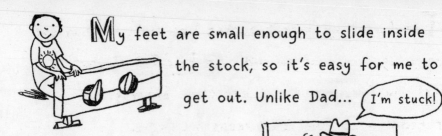

My feet are small enough to slide inside the stock, so it's easy for me to get out. Unlike Dad... I'm stuck!

Mum thinks he's joking and takes more pictures.

"NO, REALLY, RITA - I can't get OUT!"

Once Mum stops LAUGHING, she tries to help Dad, but he really is STUCK. "Can you get some HELP?" Dad wants to know.

"It's a SHAME the others aren't here to see you now!" Mum is still laughing.

"Hilarious... Help, please?"
I stay with Dad and keep him company while Mum goes to find someone.
"Can I have those crisps now?" I ask.

"Really, Tom? Now?"

"Yes, please."

"They're in my jacket pocket," he sighs. The crisps are a bit crunched up and only **PLAIN** flavour. **NOT** my favourite but I eat them anyway. Pretending to feed Dad keeps me busy...

"That's NOT FUNNY, TOM!" Dad says as I take the crisps away.

"It is quite FUNNY, Dad," I say. We've attracted quite a lot of attention from people coming out of the cafe.

Ha! Ha! Ha!

"Where's your mother?" Dad wants to know.

"Here she comes with the man who sold us the tickets," I tell him as they get closer.

"There's ALWAYS ONE... Hello again, sir," the man says.

"We must stop meeting like this," Dad sighs.

Once he gets FREE, Dad gets a round of applause from all the people watching.

"Thank you – and now for my next trick," he jokes. The man who helped Dad doesn't LAUGH at all.

"No more incidents today, I hope, sir?" he says sternly.

"Let's hope not," Mum answers for him.

"Can we EAT NOW?" I want to know.

"It's 14:15, less than TWO hours before we _have_ to leave for the **disco.**" But Mum's not listening – she's trying to ring Delia.

"WHERE ARE THEY? You'd think we would have found them by NOW."

I start pulling Mum's arm in the direction of the cafe so she gets the hint.

OK, Tom.

The cafe is still a little bit crowded and when we get to the counter, the lady serving says,

"I'm SO SORRY ... we've run out of HOT FOOD. It's been so busy!"

 "Brilliant! What DO you have then?" Mum sighs.

"They've got CAKE!" I point out.

 "It does look good..." Dad agrees.

"We've got a few tuna sandwiches left,"

the lady says.

"Can I have CAKE?" (I'm not having tuna.) Dad and I have cake, Mum has a sandwich and we all have juice. When Dad goes to pay, he says,

HOW MUCH? because it costs a lot.

187

Chocolate cake

My chocolate cake is worth it,
though.

Mum says I can have something "proper"
to eat later on. We find a table and Dad is still
grumbling. "This better be good cake for
THAT price!"

Mum offers me a bite of her sandwich and I pull a
face. "No, thanks."

Then, before I can say, "NO!" she reaches
over and takes some of my cake!

Huh?

"It looks delicious!"

I eat the rest of it really fast so she
can't have any more. Mum and Dad seem
to be chatting a lot instead of eating, and
TIME is ticking on. I TAP my WATCH to
make a point.

"I bet Delia's taken them to the MAZE and
that's why we haven't seen them,"
Dad is saying.

I'd forgotten about the maze. "Can I go in the MAZE? We could look for the others at the same time," I suggest with a mouth full of cake.

"So much for a FAMILY day out," Mum sighs.

"Let's all go to the MAZE, then ... together. It won't take long," I say, hopefully. 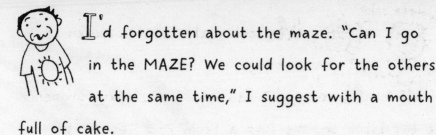 Dad gets out the map to see where it is and we follow him around the **castle** before ending up back at the cafe.

"It's THIS WAY," Dad says as we try again. There's still NO sign of the others at the MAZE, and worse still we have to pay |MORE| to go in.

Dad decides not to come with us.

 "It's cheaper and I can keep a lookout."

"OK - we won't be long."

Mum waves then follows me in.

I'd forgotten how HUGE the maze is. Mum and I walk for what seems like AGES and then my ALARM goes off, so I know it's  16:00 .

I'm getting really tired when Mum says, "I think we're LOST."

We're so LOST that we have to ring one of the bells and wait for someone to come and show us the way out.

It takes them a while to find us, but when we FINALLY do get out ...

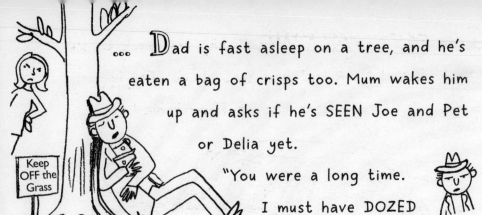

...... Dad is fast asleep on a tree, and he's eaten a bag of crisps too. Mum wakes him up and asks if he's SEEN Joe and Pet or Delia yet.

"You were a long time. I must have DOZED off," he says sleepily.

Mum tries her phone again and gets excited because she has a signal. "It's ringing...

DELIA, WHERE ARE YOU?"

While Mum's on the phone, I check to see if Dad's left any crisps. (He hasn't.)

"They're in the car park waiting for us," Mum says, which is GOOD NEWS as now I'm in a BIG HURRY.

"LET'S GO!" I shout. I don't want to be late.

I do *FAST WALKING* all the way back to the

car park and Mum and Dad just about keep up.

(I can hear them puffing behind me.)

Delia and The Wrinklies are WAITING for us.

"There you are! We missed you all day."

Then everyone starts to relive the

WHOLE trip. Which is all very well, but I

have a TROPICAL disco to get to!

So I STOP them and say,

"Can we go NOW, please?"

Then I remind The Wrinklies I'm going in

THEIR car.

Even better for me, Delia goes with Mum and Dad. "We can have a nice catch-up and I'll tell you how your Dad got stuck in the stocks," Mum says. Delia looks thrilled.

"It wasn't my fault!"

"TROPICAL **disco**," I mutter, as I'm really keen to get <u>moving</u> and everyone's still chatting. I hop in The Wrinklies' car, which is much comfier than ours. As soon as I sit down I start to feel a bit sleepy.

Granddad Joe asks if I liked the **dungeon**.

"We didn't go. We had the wrong ticket."

"Oh, what a shame," Granny Pet says as my eyes
get heavier.

Then the car begins to slow down.

"Oh dear – looks like we've hit traffic,"

she sighs.

My watch says it's now **17:00** .

I can still get to the **disco** – I might

miss a bit of it, but not much.

I decide to have a little sleep so I'm FRESH for
the TR🍍PICAL **disco**.

I get out my ticket and hold it
so I'm all READY. This **disco**
is going to be...

zzzzzzzzzz

The car comes to a complete stop.

"This doesn't look good," Granddad whispers.

I missed the

TRPICAL disc.

I'm the ONLY kid who didn't go. I know this because Marcus tells me as soon as he sees me. Derek did TRY to make me feel better on the way to school by saying,

"It wasn't as much fun without you there."

But Marcus won't stop going ON about it.

There's already a WHOLE noticeboard of pictures from the **disco** pinned up. Everyone is there and looking like they had the most AMAZING time.

Sigh...

I walk past without stopping because I don't want to be reminded of what I've missed. Kids keep saying, "Where were you?" and, "Tom, you missed out!" "It's a LONG story," I say. Then, when I sit down in class, AMY says,

"I can't believe you missed the **disco,** Tom."

   "I know."

"You were really looking forward to it."

   "I know."

Even Mr Fullerman, who's still wearing his flower garland, says, **"Did everyone have a GOOD TIME at the disco?"**

YEAH!

Sigh

It's not like I've got a REALLY good reason for missing it, either. We just got stuck in traffic and I fell asleep. Then, by the time The Wrinklies arrived at school, it was all over. I didn't even know about it until the morning. Dad had to carry me up to bed, and when I woke up the next day, I was still holding my **disco** ticket.

At lunchtime, I take a look at the photos pinned up and see what I missed.

It looks like it was FUN.

(Buster's been drawing again too. He just can't help himself.)

The WHOLE school day I have to listen to how 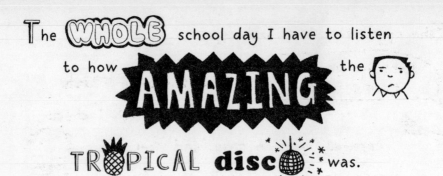 AMAZING the

TROPICAL disco was.

I get through it – just.

By the time I arrive home I'm ready to RELAX and do something to take my mind off missing out. Mum can see I'm fed up too, because she lets me watch cartoons and doesn't ask about homework or anything.

"Did you have a good day?" Mum wonders.

"It would have been BETTER if I hadn't missed out on the **disco,**" I tell her.

Even Delia's trying to be nice to me.

(Which is odd.)

She opens the door and says,

Here you go, Tom.
Have a wafer. It's not even a TRICK

wafer either, although I check

carefully just in case, and then eat

it quickly so she can't take it back.

Mum must have told Granny Mavis and Granddad
Bob about me missing the **disco,** because they
POP over as well. Granddad is showing off his
new TEETH, which are very BRIGHT.

Good as
new!

Then Granny Mavis says, "Tom, we heard things
didn't go well the other day, so we have a NICE
surprise for YOU..."

"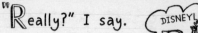eally?" I say.

"It's not DISNEYLAND, Tom,"
Mum tells me (like she can read my mind).

"It's on Wednesday evening, so be ready, OK?
We'll collect you and **D**erek too, if he wants
to come."

"I'll ask him!" I say as this is

cheering me up a LOT.

I like <u>nice</u> surprises. (Who doesn't?)

Dad comes in from his shed and

compliments Granddad on his new teeth.

"I'm sorry we missed **Crambly Castle**.
How was it?" Granddad wonders.

"**E**XPENSIVE," Dad grumbles straight away.

"It was OK," Mum adds.

"Dad got STUCK in the STOCKS like a real
criminal," I tell **THE FOSSILS**.

"Thanks for sharing that, Tom," Dad says. Granny Mavis wants the (WHOLE) family to come on Wednesday. "The MORE the merrier!"

"Even Delia?" I check.

"Of course and you can bring your vuvuzela along too."

"CAN I?" I'm liking the sound of this outing already.

"Are you sure about that, Mavis?" Mum sounds surprised.

Before anyone changes their mind, I *rush* over to let Derek know. He's very pleased to see me, and starts demonstrating how some of the teachers were dancing at the **disco.**

"You REALLY should have been there!" Derek says in mid dance.

Sprocket

Mrs Mumble clapping

Marcus pogoing

"Next time I WILL be, and THAT'S a promise."

I'm still not EXACTLY sure what **THE FOSSILS** have in mind for us all, but having something to look forward to is exciting.

Maybe it's tickets to see **DUDE 3** ?
(Not with a vuvuzela.)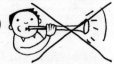

A meal out?
(Not with a vuvuzela.)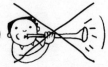

A trip to the cinema?
(Not with a vuvuzela.)

WHAT could it be?

I head off to bed still wondering what we're going to be doing. It's not long now before I find out...

My vuvuzela

IT'S HERE
WEDNESDAY'S EPIC ADVENTURE

Derek and I are waiting in the front room while Mum and Dad are upstairs changing. I'm wearing my sunshine T-shirt and Derek has his Hawaiian shirt on. We're watching TV and drawing at the same time (with our **SECRET AGENT PENS**).

"Do you really have no idea what we're doing?" Derek asks me.

"It's a SURPRISE," I say.

"Is it educational?"

"I don't think so. Unless it's a concert with vuvuzelas!"

"Will there be food?"

"Yes, lots apparently. That's the one thing I do know."

"Will your granddad be wearing a WIG?"

"Probably. Or a HAT, maybe?"

"Do you think they're SPIES?" Derek wonders.

"No, I don't think so. But can I borrow your SPY BOOKS now you've read them?"

"Sure, I'll bring them to school."

Mum and Dad are taking AGES to get ready. Delia ISN'T coming because she says she's had enough FAMILY for a while. Then we hear Mum shout,

Come on, you two. LET'S GO!

"TA-DAH!" Mum says.

"What do you think?" Dad asks.

"Is THIS the surprise?" I want to know, looking at their outfits.

"NO, silly. Come on, you two, let's go back in time!" Mum says and starts clicking her fingers.

Vuvuzela.

Delia comes down to wave goodbye, and even she's wearing a different pair of sunglasses.

BYE!
Have a wild time. Don't be LATE!
I won't miss you.

We get into the car and I recognize the way we're driving.

"All your grandparents are already there," Mum says. When we pull up outside the LEAFY GREEN OLD FOLKS' HOME, I see a BIG poster outside, and EVERYTHING starts to make sense.

"I think I know what we're doing now," I tell Derek. "Look..."

Dad dancing

Mum sway

Mum and Dad are dancing already, which is embarrassing. "As you missed out on the TR🍍PICAL **disc🪩**, we thought you'd enjoy coming to THIS one!" Mum tells us.

"It's going to be **DISCOTASTIC!**" Dad says.

We watch them dance into the old folks' home.

　　"Sorry..." I say to Derek.

"It's fine. Come on, I'll show you how Mr Fullerman danced. It was HILARIOUS," Derek says. (That's why he's my best friend.)

I take a selection of fruit 🍬🍬 chews round to The Wrinklies after school to say thank you for the presents AND the BRILLIANT time I had yesterday. ☺ Also, Granny Pet told me she'd NEVER had a fruit chew before, so I'm EXCITED to change her LIFE. (It will.) ☺

The LAST person I'm expecting to see when the door opens is DELIA, who helps herself to a chew before I can stop her.

"My FAVOURITE! Thanks, Tom."

"HEY, that's not for you! What are you doing here?" I ask as Delia walks past me.

She has a BIG bag on her back, which is not like Delia at all.

"Never you mind. See you at home. Thanks for the chew!" she says.

I go inside and The Wrinklies are pleased to see me. The fruit chews are a success – they think they're DELICIOUS!

Mmmmmm

"Told you!" I say.

Then I ask about Delia. "WHAT was she doing here?" I want to know.

"Delia just came to say hello and borrow some of our travelling kit for when she goes away," Granny Pet explains, still chewing.

"She's going away? When? Where?"

"I'm not sure – you should ask Delia. We've been having lots of chats about ADVENTURES lately."

"I will ask her," I say and offer the rest of the chews. This is BIG news that I don't think Mum or Dad know about YET.

Back at the house, I wait until we're all eating dinner together (which doesn't happen very often during the week).

Mum says, "I had such a GOOD time at the **SLIPPED DISCO** - Teacup Tony was a REVELATION!"

"Wasn't he?" I've mostly only seen him asleep!" Dad says.

"Now you know why he's SO tired all the time!" Mum says.

I wait for the right moment to say, "It's going to be LOVELY and quiet here very soon..."

"Why's that, Tom?" Mum wonders.

"Is your vuvuzela broken?" Delia asks.

"**NO**, but you're going AWAY, so it will be  quiet then," I tell EVERYONE.

"You're going AWAY?" Mum and Dad both say together.

"Here we go," Delia sighs. "I'm NOT going away for very **long**," is all she wants to tell us.
But Mum and Dad want to know more, so I helpfully remind Delia all about the travelling <u>kit</u> and BIG BAG she borrowed.

"You NEVER carry bags as big as that. AND you stole a fruit chew, too," I add.

"Is that what you've been talking to Pet and Joe about, then? Travelling?" Mum asks.

"Yes and NO," Delia says. "I did borrow some stuff, but only because I'm going away ...

... to a MUSIC FESTIVAL, which is only TWO hours away. So you can STOP worrying now," Delia tells us.

 "Is that ALL?" I say.

"Well, that's OK, then. Who's playing?" Dad asks.

 "Just **DUDE 3** and lots of other bands that are really good too."

"You need to let us know when you're going and WHO you're going with!" says Mum.

I shout,  "She's going with ME! I'm coming to see **DUDE 3** at a FESTIVAL!"

 "THAT will never happen, little brother," Delia tells me. "I'm going with Avril and some friends. There's NO WAY you're coming with us."

(That's what SHE thinks.)

 "I haven't been to a FESTIVAL in years," Dad says. Mum asks Delia a few more questions, and I say,

"CAN WE GO TOO, PLEASE? PLEASE!"

Dad says, "We'll see."

I have a few months to work out a way to get me, Derek and Norman to this MUSIC FESTIVAL.

"We'll see" isn't a "No", so that's a start.

I'm definitely up for another

 EPIC ADVENTURE!

Meanwhile, back at HAIRTASTIC...

Did you spot Buster's handiwork?

ARMADILLO

If you're wondering where some of
my ideas come from, now you know!

I got to hold a REAL armadillo
and it did have an odd whiff about it,
but I did think maybe that's what
it thinks about ME?

←—Hair

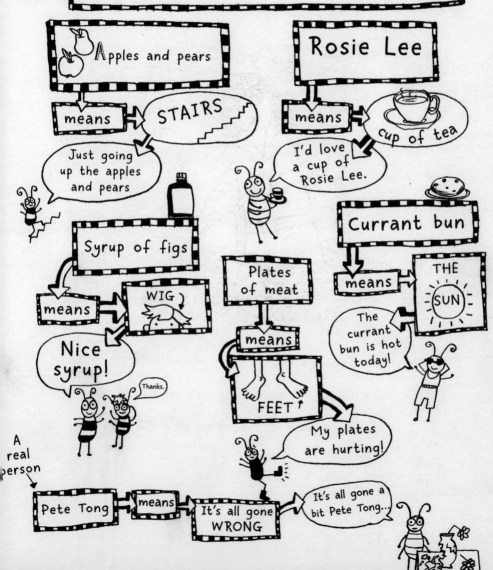

How to Make a Paper
PALM TREE

(<u>So</u> useful.)

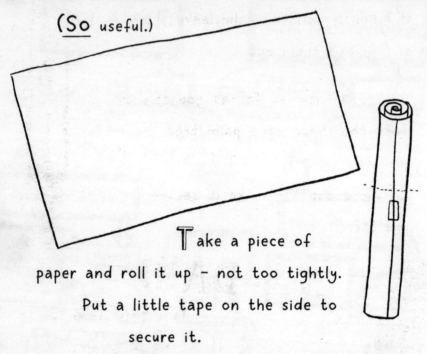

Take a piece of
paper and roll it up – not too tightly.
Put a little tape on the side to
secure it.
Then carefully cut with scissors down through
all the paper strips like this ➡

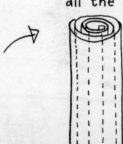

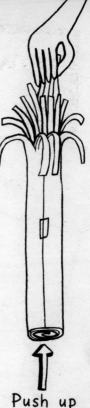

T hen hold the centre of the paper and gently pull the palm leaves up and spread them out.

Pull them as far as you can to make the shape of a palm tree.

Use more tape to make it secure, and then...

Push up

←TA-DAH!

Your palm tree is

DONE!

THE SECRET MESSAGE IS...

THE NEXT BOOK IS OUT MAY 2018

When Liz ✎ was little ♀, she loved to draw, paint and make things. Her mum used to say she was very good at making a mess (which is still true today!).

   She kept drawing and went to art school, where she earned a degree in graphic design. She worked as a designer and art director in the music industry 🎸, and her freelance work has appeared on a wide variety of products.

   Liz is the author-illustrator of several picture books. Tom Gates is the first series of books she has written and illustrated for older children. They have won several prestigious awards ⭐, including the Roald Dahl Funny Prize, the Waterstones Children's Book Prize, and the Blue Peter Book Award. The books have been translated into forty-one languages worldwide.

Visit her at www.LizPichon.com